MODEL CITIZENS

Riding for a Fall

by Henry Pepper

A Sense of Place Publishing 2013

ISBN-13: 978-1-4566-2014-1

For Anita

TABLE OF CONTENTS

THE KODAK

And lo the darkness fell upon Los Angeles.

On the coast, the blood red sun sank beneath a hazy Pacific horizon.

Downtown a cold wind pushed its way through the concrete canyons, stirring the few Christmas decorations remaining on shop fronts.

Uptown the closer drivers got to the Hollywood Hills, the more detours and police security checkpoints they encountered that Friday night.

From the corner of the North Highland and Hollywood Boulevards, hundreds of stretch limousines were backed up from the Kodak Theatre.

Inside the brightly shining Kodak, visibly excited A-listers, dressed as if winter had not yet arrived in the United States of America, hurried through the Theatre's tiered interior in search of their seats.

Out the front of the Kodak lobby, dozens of television cameras, hundreds of news and entertainment photographers and the fleet of glistening limousines combined to create the illusion that anything was possible.

Paparazzi photographers cat-called the Who's Who of World Fashion as clusters of the famous and infamous alighted onto the plush red carpet.

Intricately dressed fashion designers from London, Milan, New York, LA, Paris, Tokyo, San Francisco and beyond. Hundreds of picture-perfect models and their lovers. Fashion agents. Actors. Hollywood film producers. Celebrities. Bloggers. Journalists. Executives. Wannabes.

Every 90 seconds, like clockwork, limousine doors swung open and another cluster of photographers' flashes exploded.

The very air they breathed was loaded with great expectations. The beautiful people posed for the cameras, creating a glamorous logjam if they lingered too long in front of their favourite photographers.

Beyond the cameras and shouting journalists, stood a small crowd of cold, windswept onlookers, genuine fans, neither slim nor beautiful, who waved at their favourite celebrities from a cordoned off viewing area.

Inside the Kodak, the world famous auditorium echoed with a thousand conversations. Giant video screens, sandwiched between Estee Lauder logos and a sky blue backdrop, adorned the glittering rectangular stage.

As the audience slowly found their seats, a collage of fashion clips played on the screens, priming the audience for American network television's live coverage of the 2009 Estee Lauder International Modelling Awards.

The repeating films highlighted the 12 models who had made it into the finals, pouting and touting, in a cascading fast-edit style that accentuated the cut, look and fit of designer fashion.

Depeche Mode's *Question of Time* rocked the theatre:

"I've got to get to you first
Before they do
It's just a question of time."

It was almost show time!

The audience murmured expectantly as the film loop finished, the music faded, the Estee Lauder logo came up on the big screens and the house lights dimmed.

Bathed in a lilac spotlight, the Master of Ceremonies, dressed in a single-breasted black Armani suit, crisply pressed white Jean Paul Gaultier shirt, a black bow tie and two-tone Spectator shoes, looked like an escapee from a 1970s James Bond film. He emerged from behind the curtains at the rear of the stage in a puff of pink smoke.

The primed audience roared with approval.

The M/C, known universally in the business only by his first name, Branson, glided past a floating steel cage suspended from the ceiling that contained two adolescent white tigers.

The muscular cats growled as Branson passed. The audience, as instructed during the warm up, gasped as the house cameras zoomed in to show a close up of their teeth.

Branson took a startled step backwards, clutched at his chest in mock shock, then smiled and bowed at the elegant cats. He skipped into a walk and headed for centre stage.

All eyes were on Branson for all the wrong reasons. There had been some snide comments in LA gossip columns over the years about his profound love of martinis, but it was only recently that his drinking issues had become a big deal.

Earlier that very Friday, a nasty *Los Angeles Times* gossip columnist had reported that Branson had made a booking at the Betty Ford Clinic for the day after the Awards.

Branson's publicist had, during a morning of mild hysteria, put out an angry denial, only for an enterprising *Good Morning America* reporter doing a stint inside Betty Ford to confirm half an hour later that Branson had indeed made a booking.

The broadcast makeup team had done an award-winning job of powdering over the tell-tale facial signs that he had fulfilled his pledge to attend every single pre-Awards party held over the festive season.

Stopping at the Estee Lauder-branded podium, Branson smiled, opened his arms wide and tapped the microphone theatrically.

"Hello everyone and welcome to the magnificent Kodak Theatre here in Los Angeles. We have a truly-special event to share with you tonight, the 10th Estee Lauder International Modelling Awards."

The extroverted Californian audience, responding to prearranged signals, once more roared with delight.

Images of famous models "bigging it up" on the catwalks of Milan, New York, Paris and Tokyo filled the screens.

Depeche Mode's *Enjoy The Silence* thumped the air:

"All I Ever Wanted
All I Ever Needed
Is Here
In My Arms."

Branson pivoted on his heels, hoping that the endorphins generated by his morning session at the Hollywood Gym were beginning to kick in.

And with that, the live show began. The 12 Estee Lauder contestants strutted out onto the Kodak runway - one by one - flaunting impossibly skimpy designer lingerie.

Right from the start, the Kodak crowd was getting involved, clapping along with the sound track as the models delivered their best moves in outlandishly expensive undergarments.

From above the catwalk, a diffusion cloud of Breise Focus and Kino Parabeam lights flattered all they caressed. Kino flathead soft lights lined the front and sides of the runway to ensure that every parading contestant looked her best.

The high-energy opening segment concluded with 12 pouting models forming a semi-circle in front of a huge Estee Lauder logo projected onto the blue screen behind the stage.

Branson closed his arms, breathed as deeply as his previous month of nightclubbing permitted and clasped his hands together. As he gestured toward the podium, the audience and the stage, Branson caught sight of himself in one of the many stage mirrors and was relieved to see the makeup appeared to be holding.

He pointed approvingly towards the beaming group of young women.

"Aren't they something? It's my great pleasure to be sharing tonight with you all ..."

Branson, the heir to a circus dynasty and immersed in the theatre business all his life, milked the audience with an expectant grin.

"As we discover which model has captured the heart and spirit of the world of fashion this year ..."

He swept his hands forward and waved enthusiastically at Alexa Chung and her fashionista friends in the first tier VIP boxes.

"This is the big one for the global fashion industry, folks!" he reminded the audience.

Pink's *Get The Party Started* danced out of a wide wall of Klein + Hummel RX240 N speakers and matching RB480 S sub-woofers.

"I'm coming up, so you better get this party started
Making my connection as I enter the room
Everybody's dancing and they're dancing for me."

The screens darkened as the parade rhythmically morphed from lingerie to spectacular designer gowns.

The models, who had been entering and leaving the stage in a perpetual circle of motion, finally came to rest beside Branson in three small groups.

The 12 contestants came from different parts of the globe and, together, presented an eclectic sample of the human form. Tall. Petite. European. African. Asian. Brunette. Blonde. Redhead.

Most of the models wore their professional catwalk faces, but two of the striking women featured on camera exchanged fleeting unscripted smiles.

The brunette and blonde's brief intimacy was magnified on the screens scattered throughout the auditorium.

A titter of whispers shot around the room.

Almost everyone in Los Angeles had heard gossip about the two models predicted to win the evening's event. In the run up to the "Estee Lauders," every gossip columnist and melodramatic entertainment reporter in the USA had asked what the Awards would do to their rumoured affair.

No one could prove the pair were lovers. Then again, they could not disprove it either.

As no one had denied a romance was happening, the media story had run and run. Would a win for either one of them, and the tens of millions of dollars in contracts that would flow from it, destroy their relationship?

After all, LA's fashion pundits had repeatedly speculated, there could be only one winner in this very public battle.

Branson smiled and raised his right arm before approaching the nearest group of models.

The lone Californian contestant, the strawberry blonde, Joanne Hart, stood tall at the centre of the group. She winked seductively at Angela Durand, the French brunette standing next to her.

Joanne's blonde hair was cut fashionably short. A gold and diamond David Webb necklace around her neck, a crimson Alaia evening dress hugged her beach girl physique, crimson L'Oreal gloss highlighted her plump inviting lips and metallic black Louboutin heels lifted her head and shoulders above the other models in the group. A post-modern siren with sparkling blue-eyes and an infectious smile, Joanne was buxom and curvaceous yet LA slim and stood around 5 foot 10 inches tall.

Angela Durand had long silky brunette hair, big brown eyes and soft-skinned creamy European features highlighted by Estee Lauder Apricot Scrub. Her physique was yoga-toned and thin. She stood 5 foot 3 inches tall.

On this night of nights, Angela wore a short Rodarte stretch-lace black dress, sheer black Rive Gauche silk stockings, red Shiseido lipstick drew the eye to her beautifully proportioned face and loud red Gucci heels complimented her gown. A red silk ribbon held her long hair neatly in place, a thin silver Chopard necklace and peace sign hung around her neck. Angela's introverted retro look and sunny personality were all designed to melt the hardest of hearts. And judging by the fascinated response of the glitterati spread out in the auditorium before her, she was succeeding.

Branson floated across the floor to stand in the middle of this group of models. He threw his left arm casually over Angela's shoulder, his right arm around Joanne's waist and the trio smiled in-synch for cameras 3 and 4. The M/C posed in a way calculated to capture the envious interest of every red-blooded male watching the broadcast on TVs in lounge rooms, bars and clubs all round the world.

"History clearly demonstrates that tonight's winner of the 2009 Estee Lauder International Modelling Awards will become the International face of the fashion industry in the years ahead," Branson touted.

He stepped back and waved as Angela and Joanne, hands on rhythmic hips, walked the 12 models off stage.

Branson spun back to face the audience and excitedly pumped the air.

"Here we go folks, it's show time!" he gushed. The screens showed film of the models pirouetting in boho-style cheesecloth shirts, tie-dyed skirts and swimwear. Joanne sported a barely there silver Aquarella Artemis bikini, as she stood bare-foot in a lush forest location, with a waterfall behind her. Grateful young men grinned at her through the cascading water.

Joanne spun around, beamed invitingly in front of the hypnotic water and paused.

Then up flashed a classically framed shot of Angela standing on a beach of golden sands, wearing a yellow La Blanca Shirr one-piece swimming costume and wide-brimmed crème sun hat. She smiled as if she was innocent and happily splashed her feet in the ocean's crystal blue water.

As the clip ended, the audience was full of excitement and anticipation. Branson stepped forward as the screen dimmed and spun around to face the room in a move that he hoped displayed his athletic form.

The screens showed a sassy young reporter standing outside the Kodak. With prompting from the event producer, Branson spun back to face the reporter and camera 5.

"We'll get back to our contestants soon but right now we're crossing to our reporter, Terri-Lee Wilson, for a report from the red carpet. What's happening, Terri-Lee?"

Terri-Lee, blonde, vivacious, petite, stood in her Reiss Sonia little black dress, black Blahnik heels and orange Shiseido lippy at the exact spot where the red carpet met the reception area.

There was an oversized ABC microphone in her tiny right hand.

"It's real busy out here, Branson!"

Behind her, British actor Hugh Grant could be seen exiting from a black limousine in a dark Ralph Lauren suit combo. He was conjoined with a red-headed woman in a black Paul Poiret micro-mini-skirt, Gucci stretch lace top with satin trim and crème Silvio Rossi pumps. The camera followed the pair to the lobby where an usher greeted them with an exaggerated thespian bow. The crowd called out excitedly. Ever the professional, while doing his shy-little-boy flirt routine, Hugh made sure the photographers had a clear shot of his best profile.

"As you can see Branson, the stars have come out tonight for *the* most highly-regarded awards in world fashion," Terri-Lee said breathlessly. The screens switched to an exterior shot. Limousines were queued-up-as far as camera 6 could see. At the front of the queue, a bunch of botoxed 90s soap opera stars alighted. As their dated sartorial style and designer hats looked tragically out of place, the telecast vision quickly switched back to the smiling ABC reporter.

"I'm hoping to talk with Super Models Kate Moss and Helena Christensen a little later on but, for now, it's back to you Branson," Terri-Lee continued as she wound up the live cross.

The crowd surrounding Terri-Lee cheered as the telecast vision switched back to the interior of the Kodak.

Branson fiddled with his earpiece while beaming into camera 1. The audience applauded and once again Branson milked the moment.

"Thank you, Terri-Lee. We'll look forward to speaking to you again a little later in the show," the M/C said and performed last year's dance-step as he grinned into camera 2.

"Don't go away folks, we meet 12 of the most gorgeous women on earth, right after these important messages."

Choreographed images of the models in bikinis, splashing in a heart-shaped swimming pool, switched to a commercial for Estee Lauder's latest anti-wrinkle skin care range.

Inside the auditorium, the giant back screen faded to purple inscribed with white and yellow flowers. The 60s were back in fashion.

At the entrance to the Kodak parking station, two sensibly dressed women were work-shopping parking rage. They yelled at each other and sounded their horns while aggressively trying to manoeuvre their late model Mercedes coupes past each other.

Neither woman would concede. A long-haired parking attendant, dressed in soiled blue jeans and a red and black flannel shirt, appeared and surveyed the narcissistic scene. He shook his head, shrugged and walked slowly back to his office. He flicked the door shut behind him, turned Eminem's *Kill You* up loud and plonked his un-shined brown boots up on a paper strewn desk.

Inside the larger car, a silver Mercedes S63 AMG, sat Giselle Richter MBA, Chief Executive Officer of the Estee Lauder cosmetics corporation. To her subordinates she was universally known as 'The Gale.' Like a strong wind, you could always hear her coming and, like a hurricane, she seldom delivered good news.

Dressed in a brown Sanders wide leg jump suit and matching brown jacket, her prized Stuart Weitzman Retro Rose pumps co-ordinated with deceptive soft-pink Estee Lauder lipstick, Giselle jutted out her big square jaw, spotted a gap and accelerated past her opponent with tyres squealing.

Finding a vacant parking spot, The Gale raised the middle finger of her left hand through the driver's window as her vanquished opponent drove past with horn blaring. Giselle had already "made it" and, as far as she was concerned, the more people who knew it the better. Before exiting the Merc she checked her phone and her hair, layering on more lipstick. Giselle clicked her key ring to lock the door and strode to the elevators, smiling.

"Life is full of little triumphs," she thought as she moved forward toward the bright lights.

Just two hours earlier, even more ruthless ambition had been on display in the models' styling room deep inside the Kodak Theatre.

The self-absorbed reality that coexists with the glamour and polished theatre of fashion - the image so perfectly portrayed on catwalks, glossy magazine covers, stages and TV screens everywhere - was clearly visible during preparations for the Estee Lauder Awards telecast.

The 12 finalists were in various stages of undress. Aretha Franklin's *Good Times* played on a Bose iPod dock and an armed female security officer, bored by the constant preening of her charges, sang along.

"Get in the groove
And let the good times roll
I'm gonna stay here
Until I soothe my soul."

Several casually dressed models stood marooned in the middle of the room, surrounded by support staff in black and white Estee Lauder uniforms. Next to them was a catering station, with two cooks resplendent in white French-style chefs' hats and jackets. Both ends of the station were covered with dozens of red roses in vases. The scene was discreetly watched over by a handful of security people and seriously obsessed fashionistas who surveyed the field and whispered knowingly into their cell phones.

Other models, including Angela and Joanne, sat at vanity stations garnished with red and yellow orchids flown in from Singapore.

Hannako, a dark-haired Eurasian girl, sat barefoot in a purple and black Christopher Kane sleeveless velvet dress and chatted happily with her boyfriend on an iPhone. Next to her, a blonde, wearing a silver Herve Leger metallic bandage dress, pretended to read a book on Kabbalah truths.

In the corner, another attention-seeking blonde girl, in a long white Alexander Wang pullover shirt and matching white Jean Yu knickers, had adopted the salute the sun yoga posture in front of her station.

Next to her, a painfully thin brunette model, wearing a large Nordstrom Asymmetrical Straw hat, blue Calvin Klein jeans with a double-prong belt and purple Haute split sleeve blouse, chewed on a lettuce leaf and stared thoughtfully into space.

The biggest attention seeker of them all was Jenna Cheney, an anorexic blonde with a reputation for exploding at all the wrong moments. A "troubled" soul, Jenna was hated by the other models for her lack of professionalism but she honestly believed if a subject didn't involve her it was unimportant.

"I would not bother to read a book I had not written," the unpublished model had told *Marie Claire* magazine during a notorious 2005 interview.

Jenna was annoyed at the muted response she had received five minutes earlier when she had breathlessly announced to her fellow competitors that the previous night she had learnt, in a dream, that she would win the 2009 Awards.

It was a sign from god, a prophecy, it was written in the stars, she was going to live happily ever after. Jenna was "like, totally certain" of it.

She had a vision of herself, bathed in the bright lights, stepping up onto the same stage that had hosted so many glittering Oscar ceremonies and graciously accepting the award while smiling lovingly at the audience. The crowd's response, as predicted by Jenna, could only be described as unprecedented. She thanked each and every one of her co-competitors for their support, their loyalty, their friendship and kindness.

The other models had burst into spontaneous applause, which then spread like a wildfire throughout the auditorium.

Jenna dreamt she had thanked her father, her Uncle Dick, everyone at Estee Lauder, all her "real special" Hollywood friends, the makeup artists, the designers and the "wonderful" Branson. There had been no hint of envy. Everybody was "so-oh" happy for her. But then, sadly for the deluded mannequin, Jenna woke up.

Back in a less cheery reality, Jenna was only half dressed as she sat and sulked at her Kodak station. She was topless and her Dolce & Gabbana denim mini skirt was tucked into the back of her red Calvin Klein knickers.

Most men would have been impressed. Her associates were not.

Without warning, Jenna, the brooding blonde princess, jumped out of her chair, screamed at a stylist and chased her into the middle of the room.

Angela Durand and Joanne Hart sniggered as the femme fatale lurched past their relatively private dressing stations in one corner. Angela wore a tangerine hand painted Mitch Mitchell jacket and black Pearl stockings. Joanne perfectly filled a well-cut red Bordelle baby doll. Their hair was wet and matted, their faces not yet made-up. Their perfect complexions shone.

Joanne leant over and whispered something into Angela's ear.

Her wet hair gently cascaded across Angela's left cheek, brushed her nose, and then slid across her face.

Joanne nodded her head vigorously. "Trust me," she said emphatically.

Angela pushed her upper body forward and shook her head. A thin Chopard silver chain necklace and the peace sign it carried bounced lightly up and down against her perfectly toned skin.

Joanne smiled and kissed her on the lips.

Angela giggled. She crossed and uncrossed her legs. Her face relaxed and she pressed her hands together, Buddhist-style, in front of her face.

"Ooooooohh, I hope so Joey," she replied with warmth in her voice.

Jenna flounced across the room again, still screeching, still topless. For the first time, Angela noticed a small black skull-and-crossbones tattoo just below Jenna's left nipple.

All eyes in the room turned to watch as an older Australian model, Ellen, rose purposefully from her ergonomically designed chair to confront Jenna.

"What the fuck is this? Amateur hour?" Ellen yelled and strode straight towards Jenna.

Dressed in a full black Zandra Rhodes couture dress, chunky silver Hip Hop King dollar necklace, red L'Oreal lipstick and red Cole Haan Chelsea pumps, her long blonde hair held back by a red Tasha head wrap, Ellen was well-regarded by Joanne for her no-nonsense personality.

"Shut it Jenna, enough of your bimbo noise, some of us are actually trying to work," Ellen growled and waved her arms about impatiently in front of the princess.

Jenna sneered, picked up a glass of Perrier water from a silver tray on the station beside her and threw the fluid over the front of Ellen's dress.

There was instant uproar in the increasingly crowded room.

All eyes were on the antagonists. They didn't have to wait long. After surveying her thoroughly soaked dress, Ellen picked up a jug of Perrier and emptied its contents over Jenna's head, then pushed her firmly backwards. Jenna crashed into a vacant makeup station, knocked over a vase of orchids and ended up lying on top of the station with her head down, mouth wide open and her hair a sodden mess.

Joanne laughed. Angela shook her head. The rest of the models in the change room giggled at the decisive conclusion to the melodrama before turning back to their primary focus, the mirror.

Humiliated, Jenna got up and started to walk back to her station. Angela pointed at her. "Your behaviour is not very professional, yes?"

Joanne snorted derisively. "You're so-oh not happening, Jenna. Face it, you're just too old for the modelling game."

Jenna frowned as Ellen added "she's a fucking dinosaur."

Joanne warmed to the theme. "You're so-oh last-year girl, why else do you think that loser Adam would hire you?"

Ellen laughed so hard she started to cough.

"You're way too kind Joey," she shouted and pointed at her now cowering opponent. "She's so last decade! It's all over for her."

Jenna, faced with humiliation, Chinese-whispers and smirks as the only outcome of her tantrum, burst into tears and ran out of the room. The head of security immediately followed her.

Ellen stood in front of Joanne dripping. "Look at what that dumb bitch has done to me," she complained. "How long before show time?"

Joanne shrugged as four stylists descended upon Ellen. She waved and blew kisses towards Angela and Joanne as the team of stylists walked her off toward a vanity station at the far end of the expansive dressing room. Another larger team of stylists arrived to prepare the two girls from the Model Citizens modelling agency.

But Joanne had a more urgent agenda in mind. She held her right hand up and stopped the stylists, the dressers, and the make-up people in their tracks. She stood, grating her chair on the polished redwood floor. She cleared her throat authoritatively as she surveyed the room.

"Yo girls! It's time to get serious here. It's show time. Let's roll."

The rowdy room immediately quietened to a steady murmur of gossip. Angela patted Joanne's derrière admiringly and grinned.

Joanne opened a four-panelled black and white Japanese Tatami screen around her make-up station and waved at the attendants to leave. Nearby, a hair dryer spluttered into action.

"Give us a few minutes please ladies. Go! Now! Right now! Go!" Joanne clapped her hands three times.

The heavily laden stylists and their entourage retreated to consult with the network's Talent Manager.

Angela and Joanne were now hidden from the rest of the room by the flower-printed tatami screen and given some audio cover by a whirring symphony of hair dryers.

Joanne leant forward to Angela, held up the index finger of her left hand and placed it upon her lips. Joanne pressed her mouth real close and breathed ever so softly into her ear: "This will be the making of us, my beautiful friend," she panted sensually.

Joanne stroked Angela's thigh affectionately as she spoke. Angela blushed and flashed Joanne a little girl smile. Another hair dryer roared into action nearby.

Angela raised her voice above the din. "I wish I was as confident as you ..."

Joanne slowly seductively brought her right index finger back to Angela's lips, her eyes narrowing to a squint. She leant forward again, pressed her lips against Angela's right ear and whispered for a minute without drawing breath.

"Oooooooohh, Joey, I don't know." Angela replied nervously. The smile had run away from her face. Her brow was furrowed.

Joanne glared at her younger friend, leaned back in her chair and paused before continuing.

"Where was I? Oh yeah, Adam. Adam, Adam, good old Adam fucking Verucce. Look, don't forget what he did to us in Milan girlfriend."

Angela listened and nodded self-consciously. She tilted her head forward; crossing and uncrossing her perfectly toned legs.

Again, Joanne leant in close. A precocious smirk passed her face. She straightened her posture, pulled her Bordelle lingerie down a little before tugging at her left ear lobe.

"Don't forget, that was only 18 months ago," Joanne exclaimed with feeling.

Angela nodded in agreement.

"Then there were his 'clients' in Paris during that storm."

Joanne exaggerated a shudder and thumped her vanity station with a clenched left fist.

Angela scowled and slowly shook her head. "Imbeciles. Cretins. Dismal leetle men." She wiggled her left little finger as she spoke. Joanne grinned and nodded. "So true, Ang," she added and slapped her thighs with both hands, thoroughly amused.

"He thought that was oh-so funny at the time, the scheming little faggot. Didn't he?" she continued.

Angela nodded in agreement. Joanne softly mimicked an effeminate male voice. "Do you wanna keep your contracts, girls?"

Angela rolled her eyes. "Cochon, er, such a pig, Joey."

Joanne laughed. "We both know how pathetic these smug-married-Alpha-males are when their dream-worlds are suddenly threatened. You do remember that creep Senator Richie, don't you Ang?"

Angela nodded and then gently shook her head with contempt. "Remember how quickly he turned from tough guy to tears and cash payments after the DVD arrived?" Joanne asked her friend.

Angela nodded again and a mischievous grin spread across her flawless face. She gently tapped her thighs with both hands. She looked Joanne in the eye and they both laughed triumphantly. Angela reached out and tenderly stroked the right side of Joanne's face.

"Who could forget such awkward circumstances?" she replied.

The pair giggled. Joanne smiled reassuringly and threw a fraternal arm around Angela's shoulder. "Who could forget such unpleasantness?" Angela asked her friend with just a hint of bitterness.

Joanne laughed brutally, leant forward, put her right index finger to her friend's lips again and whispered in Angela's right ear. As she spoke, Angela's facial expression changed from amused to shocked. She gently pushed Joanne away. Angela's brow creased and she stared off into the middle distance.

"Non Joey. Don't tell me anything else ... so much bad karma will flow from this idea," she whispered in a worried tone. Angela's voice cracked as she spoke. Her hands wrapped tightly around her waist. She moved her head rhythmically back and forth.

"Ooooooohh non, Joey, non! It is not right, yes."

Joanne motioned for Angela to turn down the volume of the conversation. "Oh spare me the amateur dramatics, darling."

Joanne stared piercingly into the younger woman's eyes, sliding her head right up close and personal.

"It did not bother you last time, French girl," she muttered aggressively.

Angela paused in momentary reflection. "Or the time before that ..."

"Look, here's the thing. Adam is making a fortune these days. He's got a ready to wear range in Walmart this season for fuck's sake," Joanne noted in disbelief.

"He might whine about it but he will pay us. He's got no choice. His wife would remove his cojones if she found out."

Joanne continued the close-range staring. Angela blinked first, looked downward and started to fidget with her hands. When she looked up again, she blushed.

"I have a really bad feeling about this, Joey. What you say, what you want us to do, it is criminal, non?"

Joanne lifted her right hand up. It hovered in front of her friend's face as her take-no-prisoners spin continued. “Relax, Ang, please. Ya’know, it’s just the way that we do things in America.”

“Non, Joey, non. Look all around the world at the trouble and suffering that is caused by the American way of doing things.”

“Everywhere you Americans go with this attitude there is trouble, yes, big trouble,” Angela replied quietly but firmly.

“Oh spare me, please. I’m not in the mood for your commie French political bullshit,” Joanne snapped contemptuously and, for a single moment, turned her head away.

“Just know this girlfriend, this is how we get things done in the States. Ya gotta hustle, ya gotta sell yourself. It’s not political, OK, it’s just business.”

Angela shook her head, dismay painted across her expressive face.

“We should be winning these awards because we are talented, yes?” she countered.

“No,” Joanne snarled ferociously. “No! Just listen. Listen carefully to me Angela Durand because I’m only going to tell you this once. It’s too late, it’s a done deal, everything is arranged, and there’s no backing out now. It’s much too late for you to change your mind.”

As Angela stared into Joanne’s eyes, the colour drained from her face as she saw that determined look she knew only too well. Joanne again held an index finger to her friend’s sweet lips.

“You might as well be pointing a gun at me,” Angela thought.

“This has got nothing to do with dumb stuff like what’s right and wrong,” the annoyed Californian continued.

“Tonight we are going to win. Tonight we are going to become Super Models. We are going to make millions and millions of dollars. That's what matters Angela Durand," Joanne whispered in a thoroughly patronising tone and smiled professionally.

Angela shook her head and frowned as two teams of stylists walked around the Tatami screen. This time, the network Talent Manager accompanied the support staff.

"Such behaviour, it is more serious than you think," Angela replied miserably. Joanne screwed up her face and shook her head as she used both her feet to push her chair away from her friend's. She raised her right hand and pointed assertively at Angela with her index finger.

"Joey ..." Angela began but before she could collect her scattered thoughts Joanne moved to finish their sensitive conversation that had suddenly acquired an unwanted audience.

"No, Ang! Let's talk about this later," she said firmly.

The ABC Talent Manager nodded her head and smiled amiably.

"Thanks for being so understanding Joanne, darling, the teams have got to get to work now. Angela, time is short, my darling, and the show must go on."

Angela stared incredulously at Joanne, who spun around in her chair, smiled at the Talent Manager and nodded at the team of stylists.

With the conversation thus terminated, Angela, still stunned, was spun around in her chair and the stylists went to work on both models with hair dryers and brushes.

THE DARK NIGHT

While neither Angela or Joanne realised it as the glamorous 2009 Estee Lauder International Modelling Awards telecast commenced, their future was taking shape ominously in Joe's Sports Bar just five kilometres away.

Joe's was a blinged-out, late night hangout where LA's professional sports people and their cronies gathered to party and scheme.

Decorated with framed National Football League, basketball and soccer memorabilia and poster pictures of various teams and individual players, the bar featured multiple large television screens, a jukebox, an eat-in restaurant section, a handful of pool and billiard tables and a few booths for patrons seeking privacy that complimented the rows of stools along the chrome and silver mirrored bar. Black tables and chairs were placed throughout the room.

Hooting patrons were watching the Estee Lauder awards on screens throughout the room. Beers were disappearing quickly. Tequila shooters hit the bar.

Two barely-dressed hostesses, in see-through micro negligees, black and red fishnet stockings and dangerously high-heeled red pumps, were serving the drinks.

Most of the male patrons were gathered in several noisy groups at one end of the bar as Gram Parsons' *Ooh Las Vegas* played.

> "Well, the first time I lose I drink whiskey
> Second time I lose I drink gin
> Third time I lose I drink anything
> 'Cause I think I'm gonna win."

Brett Farrell was slouched alone at the other end of the bar, his gigantic hands cradling his balding head. A three day growth sat upon his chin, his eyes were red and bleary, his demeanour unsteady. Directly in front of him lay three large drinks, the sport pages of a tabloid newspaper, car keys and an iPhone.

Brett wore long khaki shorts, a red Lacoste long sleeved t-shirt bearing the *Porn Star* motif and a blue and yellow LA Eagles NFL baseball cap he was wearing back-to-front.

While intensely watching the broadcast of the Estee Lauder Awards on the screen in front of him, Brett was shaking his head, muttering loudly to himself and gulping down drinks.

Several men in the nearest group, dressed in smart casual and bling styles, were looking sideways at Brett. They were trying not to be too obvious about it, whispering among themselves behind cupped-hands.

The tallest man in the group said "I guarantee you it is Mr Football." Several other members of the group disagreed. A man dressed in blue jeans, lace-up boots, a black long sleeved polo shirt and a Ford cap spoke up.

"Man, you is just playing with us. Doncha blowhard, my man."

"Playing with you? Cha," replied the tall man. "How do I know? Yo dude! I used to work for the Eagles Junior Bowl and Ivy College Leagues, that's how I know."

"OK, OK, you're the man," replied the dude. "Let me buy you a double." The tall man smiled insincerely and gave him the thumbs up with his left hand.

As the group continued stealing glances in his direction, Brett turned on his stool and stared coldly back at them.

"Who are you looking at?" he growled.

The herd of men, collectively, looked away.

Back at the Kodak Theatre, the "Estee Lauders" broadcast returned from a commercial break, somewhere past mid-point in the proceedings. It was the photo opportunity, cheesy-interview, meet-the-contender-phase. Branson had the smooth-cabaret routine down pat. His black bow tie and body language soft but firm as he stood, relaxed, at the podium.

"Welcome back everyone ..."

Branson waved at the crowd and they cheered right back at him. He savoured the massive reaction.

"Wow! What a wonderful audience you are. You deserve to give yourselves a round of applause."

Branson waved his hands like an orchestral conductor and applauded the beautiful people of Los Angeles.

The cameras showed celebrity members of the audience enjoying the atmosphere in that magnificent domed auditorium as Branson milked yet another magic moment.

"Thank you," Branson said and bowed. "Thank you," he repeated, bowing again. "Thank you."

Branson flashed his best wide smile and let the applause run until it had faded enough for him to break in.

"Can I just say, meeting each of the 2009 Estee Lauder International Modelling Awards contestants in an up close and personal kinda way has got to be my favourite part of this wonderful ceremony."

The M/C gestured to six alluring women - Miranda, FuXai, Elizabeth, Hannako, Gabriella and Amber-Jane - who were aligned to his left.

"Before the break, we met the beautiful women who make up the first group of contenders for the 2009 Model of the Year crown."

The audience responded energetically.

Branson then motioned toward a second group of six models to his right. Joanne, who stood tall and proud at the front of the queue, struggled to get her money-shot smile happening. Angela, Jenna and Ellen, all bearing their best million-dollar smiles, were also among the second group.

"Now it's time to meet the women in our second group of contestants. And, hey, who better to get things moving than the lovely Joanne Hart?"

Joanne sashayed down the runway, poised and elegant. She was brimming with confidence, her exemplary catwalk skills clearly on display as she strutted, technical issues with the smile apparently resolved.

Jenna was not smiling in the background but Branson was.

"Ladies UND gentlemen! All the way from Indian Hills, Los Angeles, would you please make Joanne feel welcome."

The crowd greeted Joanne with an enthusiastic ovation. Photographers' flashes exploded, creating a tsunami of white light that erupted like a solar flare. Branson shielded his eyes.

"Hello again, Joey," he said with a dazzling ice white smile.

Joanne and Branson, laughed, curtsied, exchanged air kisses and embraced. She smiled glowingly. He brushed her bottom lightly with his right hand.

"At 23, Joanne is clearly one of the rising stars of American modelling and some of my wisest friends tell me she has the potential to be even bigger than Kate or Stella..."

Joanne acted as if she was completely amazed at this revelation. She blinked at camera 2. Tears started to well in her doe eyes and her voice began to crack.

"Branson, how sweet of you to say that. But really, I'm just a little ol country girl who is lucky enough to be following my dreams."

"I ... I ..."

Joanne had the lip-trembling, onion-tears thing going on. Branson slipped his arm around her shoulder, smiled and paused to emphasise Joanne's well-rehearsed dramatic turn.

"Let's take a brief look at some of the career and life highlights of a name - ladies UND gentlemen - that we're surely going to be hearing a lot more about in the years ahead!"

Joanne's eyes widened as if she were even more astonished while Branson subtly checked how his makeup was holding up to the burning glare of the stage lights. "So far, so good," he thought to himself.

Joanne's 30-second package included family-video-footage of her as a nine year old ballerina dancing in tights and tiara; winning a Hollywood modelling award at 15; a brief interview with her 1979 Playboy playmate mom and Indian Hills golfer step-father saying how proud they were of her; a collage of images of Joanne storming the catwalks of New York and Paris; dressed in white and walking arm-in-arm with famous footballer Brett Farrell in a lush flower garden; and pictures of her parading Dior couture wear with Angela at an enormous Tokyo shopping mall.

Aretha Franklin's *I Say a Little Prayer* accompanied the Model Citizen's video highlights.

"My darling believe me,
For me there is no one
But you."

The compilation faded to purple with white and yellow hippy flowers. Branson grinned boyishly and gave a thumbs-up sign of approval for the audience and camera 3.

Back at Joe's Bar, the group of men - and the two hostesses - were now gathered around Brett Farrell. He was happily telling tall football tales, surrounded by dozens of full and empty spirit glasses and beer bottles.

Brett had removed his baseball cap, showing the hulking 31 year old's receding hairline. He had tattoos on his arms, neck and chest.

"So Turvey turns to him and says who scored the touchdowns anyway?"

The big name quarterback chortled loudly at his own joke and took a shot of whisky while soaking up the group's laughter - they all seemed determined to outdo each other. They'd be recounting this meeting and Brett's locker-room tales for the rest of their days.

The football star gently lifted the mini-skirt of one hostess as she turned away from the group to check a text on her phone. He lowered his head down and sniffed her bottom.

The other hostess spotted the sleaze and glared angrily at Brett. He dropped the skirt, lifted his head and raised the thumb of his huge right hand in her face. The group laughed again and Mr Football earned himself several supportive slaps on the back.

The hostess shook her head and walked away from the group with head held high. She made straight for the bar manager to make a complaint.

"He's a strange one, Turvey, that's for sure," Brett slurred as he leered at his victim's breasts.

The group of fans laughed along drunkenly. Brett looked up, noticed the hostess of choice scowling at him and winked. She looked uncomfortable, put down her drink and picked up her phone.

"Don't you think that stuff that happened with you and Thommo was pretty off-key? I mean, didn't he recruit your ass for the Eagles in the first place?" the tall man asked the LA Eagles quarterback.

A murmur of agreement rippled through the growing throng of male fans.

Brett nodded vigorously. His hands were suddenly drawn into clenched fists, his knuckles white, his jaw drawn tight, his brow lined.

The second hostess looked at a new text on her phone, glared at Mr Football, deliberately knocked her glass over on his table and made to leave the group.

As she walked away, fuming, the footballer shook his head, leant forward out of his chair and smacked her hard on the bottom with his right hand. The hostess shrieked and ran to the bar without looking back. Brett yelled after her.

"Yo, ho, get back here and wipe down my table. And bring me another bourbon while you're at it."

He shrugged to the group and picked up another drink. "Fucking skank. Sorry dude, you were saying something about Thommo?"

"Yeah buddy, like, with the two of you, united, we could not lose but, hey, since Thommo went on the injured list last season, things have not been as good as they should be."

Brett was tense. Breathing deeply through flared nostrils, his face reddened even as he unclenched his fists, the footballer launched stiffly into what looked like a poorly rehearsed public relations routine.

"Don't even mention Thommo."

He paused, looked up, sighed and slowly emptied his glass. He slammed the empty vessel down on the table.

"Yeah, I just wish it had never happened. Like, that whole scenario just haunts me, you know."

The group of men were hanging on the NFL star's every word. He stole a glance at the exposed bottom of the first hostess who was now unloading a dishwasher further up the bar. When she looked up, he winked at her, opened his mouth and wriggled his tongue about.

The bar manager walked up to the dishwasher and tried to comfort Brett's victim. He placed his hand on her shoulder and gently sought to persuade her not to call the police.

And Brett? Brett, as always, was thriving on being the centre of attention.

"Thommo's knee is good to go again. We will be unbeatable again in Super Bowl 2009 if he and Coach Hemline can just find it in their hearts to forgive me."

This was big news to the group of open-mouthed men who were, accordingly, very happy at this once in a lifetime opportunity to be NFL 'insiders.' Three of the group returned with trays of drinks. Uninvited, the footballer grabbed two glasses of bourbon off one of the trays.

"In fact, dudes, I'm certain that the 2009 Eagles are destined to be legends. I'm real sure we can be even better than the 2007 team because of what happened," Brett said.

"That's if Thommo can just forget about the issues of the past and focus on the glorious future of our football team?"

The footballer shared a cheesy grin with the group and patted the tall man on the back. "I'll be, like, real happy to have him back for Super Bowl and calling some plays from the centre."

"Hallelujah to that," said the tall man. Brett smiled and having spotted both the hostesses angrily looking in his direction, he stood up, theatrically bowed to les miserable and noisily blew a kiss their way.

The group laughed. Two balding middle-aged men in suits, loitering by the nearby pool tables, applauded and wolf-whistled at the two unfortunate women.

"I've sure learnt a lot from what happened and the commentators agree that since 2007 I've become America's greatest duel threat quarterback," Brett continued.

His audience of slack-jawed fans nodded as one.

"If the commentators are right and I'm real sure they are right, it's because I've, like, learnt to control my temper, and, yeah, you know, I have Thommo and Coach Hemline and the Eagles to thank for that."

Brett winked at the hostesses.

"I've grown a whole lot as a footballer and as a man these past two years," he claimed.

"Things can only get better for the Eagles," Brett said humbly and smiled at his drinking buddies. "Things will get better, starting with our victory in Super Bowl 2009."

"Hallelujah and amen to that. Can I buy you another drink brother?" the tall man asked.

"Yo, I'll have two bourbon doubles, my man, and be sure to tell that ho that if she wants a tip she better get right over here and wipe down my ... table," Brett yelled over his shoulder in the direction of the bar.

The group hooted as the tall man headed for the bar. Brett slammed down someone else's shot of bourbon just as Biggie Smalls' *Juicy* blasted through the room. Half a dozen of his admirers moved closer to Mr Football.

One man pulled out an iPhone.

"Can we get some pictures with you buddy?" he asked hesitantly.

"For $1000 a picture you can," Brett replied sarcastically. The group shrank back from him and he laughed.

"Hey, I was only joking guys. Take all the pictures you like."

The groupies milled around Mr Football and, two and three at a time, they toasted as others used their phones to make sure they captured permanent bragging rights from the day they met their hero.

"We can all see how much you've learnt in every game this season, you've been totally awesome buddy. You are the greatest of them all and I mean that totally 100% sincerely," said a fat bald man with a large unlit Cuban cigar in his mouth and a crème felt 10 gallon Texan hat in his right hand.

There was a group-high-fiving-scene that Brett joined in half-heartedly while reaching for another shot glass.

"Can I get your autograph?" asked the fat man. The NFL star looked blankly at him. "Sure, why not buddy," he slurred in reply.

As the fat man placed his hat upon his head and reached into his jacket pocket for a pen, there was a colourful flicker of light around the bar area as someone changed the TV channel. The Estee Lauder International Modelling Awards coverage reappeared and Joanne's smiling face immediately filled all the screens in Joe's Bar.

A couple of patrons further down the bar hooted appreciatively. Brett stiffened, his practiced plastic smile disappeared from his face, the suddenly scowling hero pushed aside the fat man and other well-wishers and lurched toward the nearest screen. The hostess he'd humiliated took one horrified glance at the crazed look on the footballer's face and, just in time, ducked down behind the bar.

The footballer issued a discordant yell and hurled a full whiskey glass at the image of his partner. The screen cracked, hissed and then disintegrated. Brett stood with his hands on his head, pulling at what was left of his hair.

A couple of members of the group of admirers coincidentally returning from the bathroom had to move quickly to avoid a violent shower of glass and electric sparks. Brett looked coldly through them like they just weren't there.

Both hostesses retreated as far away from the angry footballer as they could get within the confines of their work environment. The victim was frightened. Her colleague rummaged in her bag, pulled out a mobile phone and, after pressing a couple of buttons, started filming the LA Eagles star's bad behaviour. She carefully positioned her phone on the main shelf behind the bar.

Brett grasped his head with his hands. His head swayed from side to side. His eyes narrowed. His brow furrowed. His top lip curled. His head twitched and wobbled around.

The footballer appeared to be totally oblivious to anything around him, fixated on the bewitchingly beautiful woman on the TV screen. The two hostesses sneered at him and whispered to each other.

"Bitch!" he yelled at no one in particular. "She has ruined my life!"

The bar fell quiet for the first time that night. There was only Branson's superficial commentary droning from the surviving TVs and, beyond that, an uncomfortable silence.

A bouncer appeared, ready to do his job, but the bar manager quietly told him not to intervene.

Brett spun around, swept the drinks off the bar space in front of him and jumped toward the group, all the while haunted by Joanne's smiling face on another monitor.

All the colour had drained from his face, tears lined the footballer's dangerous eyes. His lips were moist with saliva. His eyelids fluttered. Sweat fell from his furrowed brow. He shook his head and repeatedly brought his fist down on a shelf, eventually smashing the unit away from the wall.

Most of the group of men was still standing in the midst of a human hurricane.

"Hey man can we, like, help you?" the tall man asked hesitantly.

"Bitch! The fucking Indian Hills bitch! She took me for everything. Aagggghhh," Brett roared so loud that if anyone actually walked LA's sidewalks they would have heard his primal scream from the other side of the street outside Joe's Bar.

Without warning, Mr Football viciously punched in the eye the smallest guy in the group, one of the dudes he had just been photographed with.

The bewildered victim flew backwards and crashed heavily into another group of patrons, knocking several other men over. The elbow of one of these falling men, in turn, knocked an autographed picture of the LA Eagles 2007 Super Bowl winning team off the wall. The glass cracked, the frame buckled and the market value of one of Joe's most prized collectables took a sudden dive as it hit the floor hard.

The tall man stepped back from the fray. This group of heroic men had no intention of physically challenging the mountainous and unpredictable Brett Farrell who had, by now, grabbed another couple of shot glasses and was again standing back at the bar. Sobbing like a baby.

Brett continued to fixate on the Estee Lauder telecast and self medicate with alcohol. He engaged with the hostess he had assaulted in a familiar tone, as if nothing had happened 15 minutes earlier.

"Why is she doing this to me? Please, tell me why?"

Kathy, the long-suffering hostess, snapped. She seriously thought about pulling the pistol out of her purse and putting an end to Brett's night of shame but, unfortunately for Joanne and Angela, she thought better of it.

Instead she marched up to the bar manager.

"I can't believe you won't call the police on this psycho pig. I quit. I'm out of here before I cap his ass!" she said angrily and paused, hoping her boss was going to intervene, deal with the footballer and ask her to stay. But he just stared evasively at his shoes.

"I'm out of here right now, and know this bro I'm dialling 911. It's the first thing I'll be doing when I'm safely in a cab," Kathy said assertively.

The bar manager lifted his head but would not look her in the eye as he replied: "I'm real sorry Kathy but he's just too well connected. You can call 911, I don't blame you, but I swear there ain't no-one going to do nothing to about psycho Mr Football. Not in this fucked up city."

He glared down the bar at the drunken wreck of a man and pointed.

"That low mothafucker is bigger than god."

The bar manager finally made eye contact with his best ex employee.

"What I can do is pay you triple for tonight's full shift. And because I'm real sorry to see you go like this, Kathy, if you sign a non-disclosure agreement before you leave, I'll pay three months wages into you account first thing tomorrow. Whaddya say girl?"

While Kathy nodded blankly, it was now she who avoided looking her ex boss in the eye.

"OK. Get changed and meet me in my office. I'll be there in 10 minutes," the manager said. She nodded again, turned and walked away full of disbelief.

The bar manager shook his head and pretended to survey the stock beside the main cash register.

Kirstie, the other hostess, stared intently at him from the other end of the bar.

"Fuck this," the manager muttered to himself when she finally caught his eye. He picked up the bar phone and touched three buttons. "It's Joe's. Yeah, yeah. We got a code nine going down. Send a VIP security posse down here right away." He gently placed the phone back down in its cradle and glared at Brett sitting four metres away. "Fuck you" he muttered and practiced a slow motion punch.

Kirstie walked up and kissed him lightly on the cheek. "Thank you boss," she said, and then scooted down the bar to serve the tall man.

Unaware of anyone and anything else, the footballer sobbed and continued interrogating the universe as he watched Joanne and Branson hug on the television. He noticed how comfortable and relaxed their body language was.

"Why? Why? Why?" Brett croaked.

But TV land was completely oblivious to his achy breaky heart. Joanne continued to smile ever so sweetly from the screens. Brett was transfixed and appalled as Branson's lecherous hand tenderly stroked Joanne's back with what his paranoid mind took to be a sense of familiarity.

"Aagggghhh!" the football super hero screamed again. "You'll pay for this slut, I promise. You are riding for a fall."

Half of Brett's fan club had remained at the scene of the crime. They had witnessed Mr Football's anti social behaviour first hand, yet most of them immediately excused him because of the blind filter of herd behaviour that groupies of all descriptions are so prone to.

"Typical of these uptown girls. She ditched him the moment she was famous ... It's such a tragedy, the Super Bowl is a week away and our man, Mr Football, is a fucking wreck. I mean, just look at him," the tall man noted earnestly as he returned from the bar with a tray loaded with full glasses.

"It's so wrong. It's so unfair of her," agreed the fat man who was surveying the basket case at the bar. "What the hell was she thinking of?"

"Someone from the Eagles should be talking to her," the tall man suggested, a proposition the group's body language suggested they supported. "The club should pull her fancy Hollywood ass back into line."

"Right. You're so right. The only way we are going to win Super Bowl 2009 is if Mr Football is in the zone," the fat man said. "Why aren't the Eagles on to it already?"

With the bar manager and Kirstie watching from the side lines, two tall thin bouncers wearing loose black trousers, long sleeved black shirts and black Nike sport shoes appeared at the bar on either side of Brett.

"Mr Farrell, sir, you've had enough to drink to-night. It's now time for you to leave," the taller man said in a measured, respectful tone.

The bar manager walked toward the football groupies with his arms outstretched and a plastic smile. "Gentlemen, I'm real sorry about this interruption," he said. "Please accompany me to the VIP bar where your drinks will be on the house for the rest of the night."

"You the man," the tall man said and slapped the bar manager on the back. The group collected their drinks and followed him away from the bar.

Brett jumped out of his stool. Despite being unsteady on his feet, he shaped up, in martial arts style, ready to fight.

The bar manager walked the group away from the looming confrontation.

The bouncers were relaxed in the face of Brett's aggressive behaviour. As they walked slowly and purposefully towards him, the LA Eagles star upped the ante and picked up a barstool with his solid left arm.

"Don't you losers know who I am?" he roared and lifted the stool up high in the air.

The bouncers nodded, unimpressed.

"I know who you are, sir. That's the only reason I'm not kicking your ass right now," the tall bouncer said patiently.

Brett threw the barstool at the smaller of the men in black and followed up with an impressive looking round house kick. The bouncer ducked the stool, easily stepped around the kick, smiled and continued moving into Mr Football's space. When Brett seized another barstool, the larger bouncer side kicked it straight out of his left hand.

The stool flew across the bar, cracked a large chrome mirror behind Kirstie and then, as it fell, knocked over a rack full of spirit bottles. A large bottle of Glen Fiddich smashed on the floor, washing Kirstie's feet with 15-year-old single malt whiskey.

Faced with obviously superior fighting skills, the footballer's macho bravado evaporated. Just like that. He raised his hands submissively, showing both his palms to the bouncers. His torso shrunk, his body slumped, his head jerked forward and he grinned his best boy next door smile at the security men.

Kirstie shook her head. "What a pathetic loser you are," she muttered to herself and adjusted the position of the phone camera to capture his capitulation. The bar manager returned from the VIP Bar and noticed she was filming the situation. He sent Kirstie round to "attend to" the VIPs, picked up her phone and deleted the video.

On the floor of Joe's main bar, the bouncers were now right in Brett's face.

The tall bouncer gently placed his left hand on Brett's right shoulder. "Grab your things, sir. You are leaving. C'mon, it's time to go."

For the first time in years, Mr Football did exactly what he was told. He picked up his phone and keys and pocketed them. As the bouncers escorted the surly yet passive footballer toward the door, the bar's television screens suddenly cut to a close up of Jenna being interviewed by Branson.

Brett's face sank. And right by the doorway he stopped walking. He wanted to watch the rest of the Estee Lauder International Modelling Awards broadcast. As the smaller of the bouncer's held the door open, the largest bouncer shoved him out onto the street with the palm of his right hand. He used the minimum amount of force required even though, as the adrenalin surged inside him, he really wanted to forget about being professional and sit the wise guy where he belonged: right on his ass.

"Hey C'mon, I don't want no trouble. Hey take it easy buddy, please, I've got a Super Bowl to win, OK?" Brett said dramatically, switching effortlessly into victim mode. A group of passers by stopped to watch.

On her way home Kathy had called 911 anonymously and, as a result, a Los Angeles Police Department patrol car, lights flashing and siren blaring, pulled up at the kerb. Two uniformed officers jumped out with their tasers drawn.

Upstairs, the patrons of Joe's Bar VIP lounge maintained their forensic focus on the football.

"We cannot win the 2009 Super Bowl without Mr Football. He is essential," the tall man regurgitated for the umpteenth time and the surrounding group of 10 men nodded in mute agreement. The small man, now sporting a black and bruised left eye, appeared to be searching for his best friend floating at the bottom of his whiskey glass.

Downstairs, as the bouncers stood with Brett and the cops on the street, the faulty front door finally automatically locked behind them.

Inside, the bar manager and Kirstie stood with arms crossed and frowning faces as they surveyed the wreckage strewn across the now almost empty main bar.

"You know on nights like tonight, babe, I really wonder why I bother getting out of bed at all," the bar manager said and sighed.

"I know what you mean boss," Kirstie replied and hitched up her red right stocking.

"We're closing early. The cleaners can sort this mess in the morning. Let me fix you a drink," he said with a smile.

“I’d like that,” she replied and raised her eyebrows a little.

“A triple vodka?” he asked and placed his left hand knowingly on her right shoulder.

“A triple bloody Mary, yep, that would be jest fine.” Kirstie grinned, looked into his eyes and placed her hands upon his hips as she ordered.

Uptown, the Estee Lauder Awards ceremony was reaching its conclusion. Branson was profiling Angela. She filled her black Rodarte stretch lace dress so perfectly it looked like a work of art. Her long black hair was now untied and flowed sensually down her back.

"It's time for us to have a close look at where Angela has come from and what she has been doing since she started charming the cameras of the world just a few short years ago," Branson breathlessly informed the Kodak crowd.

On the screens appeared a high definition video package of Angela's 'colourful' past as the daughter of a left wing French politician. Aretha Franklin's *Respect* was playing.

"What you want
Baby I got it
What you need
Do you know I got it?"

The audience was shown clips of Angela "overjoyed" and hugging her mother after signing her first Chanel contract; her picture on the cover of *Vogue France* as a fashionable 16 year old Iyengar yoga protégée; playing golf with her besotted father and eminent Parisians; and Angela on location in London's Battersea Park sensually modelling Agent Provocateur lingerie for a dozen photographers.

"Without doubt, at just 21 years of age, Angela Durand is already one of the world's premier photographic models," Branson gushed. "She was recently described by *The New York Times* as the face of our time."

As Branson showed camera 4 a copy of a recent issue of *Marie Claire* magazine with Angela's stunning face on the cover, Angela blushed and smiled shyly. Branson put his arm around her tiny waist.

"Thank you so much for being with us tonight, Angela. Good luck in the awards and, believe me when I say, we all look forward to seeing a whole lot more of you in the future!"

Angela performed a curtsy to the audience and flashed her best billion dollar smile at camera 3. The Kodak's capacity crowd of 3500 were charmed and thrilled and made sure she knew all about it.

"Ladies UND gentlemen!! Angela Durand!! From France," Branson announced proudly. "What a truly luscious woman from a truly special country. What a fine ambassador for European fashion and culture she is."

As the crowd roared its approval, Branson and Angela embraced, air kissed, then waved from the awards lectern to the rapturous crowd.

"Please don't touch that remote," Branson purred. "Coming up right after these important messages from our sponsors, we reveal who is the winner of the Estee Lauder International Modelling Awards for 2009!"

Branson looked approvingly at Angela and then swept both his arms outward to highlight all the contestants.

"And don't forget y'all, you can find lots of important information about Angela, about all the girls and the wonderful sponsors of tonight's special presentation on our website. The address is on your screen right now."

Meanwhile, outside Joe's Bar, the two police officers had sandwiched themselves between Brett and the bouncers.

"Look, Mr Farrell has kindly agreed to pay for all the damages and because he is obviously upset about splitting up with his girlfriend, we think you should just let the matter rest at that," the senior police officer said to the two VIP security officers.

"So because he's Mr Football, you're gonna let him off?" asked the increasingly agitated tall bouncer.

"That's not what I said, sir," the LAPD officer replied coldly.

"He's a football legend," the bouncer pointed at Brett and continued. "His dad's a football legend. Seems to me like what you're doing here is some kind of celebrity cover-up. He can do what he likes. There are no rules for him. The rest of us have to obey the law. We must live like decent ordinary people. If we acted like him, we would be arrested and locked up for sure."

The two police officers exchanged knowing looks. The junior cop nodded reassuringly to Brett. Both uniformed officers moved in closer to the angry bouncer.

The second bouncer looked down at the sidewalk, wishing he could just disappear from this career-threatening scene.

"Listen up buddy, we can take all this inside and start checking on compliance with the club's licence conditions, is that what you want?" the talking cop barked.

"You can be sure that's not what your boss wants," the 'good' cop added. "And we'll be doubly certain to check Joe's compliance with every single licence condition. Does your boss have five hours to spare buddy? Are you still going to have a job in five minutes time?"

A worried expression crossed the tall bouncers face, a light bulb had finally gone off. He was seriously out of his depth. He knew that letting testosterone talk was a big no-no in LA's more influential circles. Suddenly he realised that it was his behaviour, not Brett's, that was on display and on trial. A picture of his comfortable life flashed before his eyes. Just in time, he pulled back from the brink, saving himself and his young family from financial ruin.

He shook his head in defeat.

"I don't think that will be necessary, sir," the bouncer replied meekly. His eyes told the tale of centuries of defeat at the hands of gringo overlords who seemed to have taken particular pleasure from crushing his forebears into the dirt.

Mr Football smirked at both bouncers, then nodded to the police officers.

"Thank you," the Hispanic good cop replied and shook both the bouncers by the hand. "Case closed. We've all got better things to be doing with our time ..." And, in a whispered voice only the bouncer could hear, he concluded: "Than to waste it on assholes who were born that way and will die that way. Take a deep breath and walk away buddy. Otherwise, you will only hurt yourself and your family."

The senior officer turned back towards a clearly inebriated and preoccupied footballer.

After a slight hesitation the two high-fived, like they were old friends. And then the officer said in a most faux courteous manner: "Enjoy the rest of your evening sir. And on behalf of the people and city of Los Angeles, good luck at the Super Bowl, sir."

While the tall bouncer looked down at the ground, seemingly fascinated by a cockroach crawling out of a crumpled Coca Cola can, he was really trying to come to terms with just how little value the principles of virtue seemed to have in the real world.

The good cop stepped forward towards his football hero.

"I agree with everything my partner just said. Please give 'em hell on the weekend, sir."

Brett, his head abruptly snapped out of a drunken hallucination involving Joanne and a harem of Super Models, responded: "We'll be doing our very best, I promise you. We will never say die. Hey, why don't you guys give me your cell numbers and I'll make sure you boys get some of the best seats in the house for Super Bowl."

"We would sincerely appreciate that Mr Farrell, you are very kind," replied the senior cop.

The good cop scribbled both their numbers onto an LAPD notepad.

In a role-reversal from ten minutes earlier, the LA Eagles star rolled his eyes contemptuously at the tall bouncer and sneered.

The good cop handed him the piece of paper, Brett glanced at the detail, flashed his teeth and nodded at the two police officers. He patted the senior cop on the back, then turned and arrogantly strolled off into the dark night.

Out of sight, after he had lurched around the first corner, the untouchable footballer threw the already crumpled piece of LAPD paper into a pool of chocolate-coloured water that had formed in the gutter.

Outside Joe's Bar, the junior bouncer deployed some relationship repair tactics with the LAPD.

"Thank you for your assistance, officers. We very much appreciate your prompt response. Can I offer either of you gentlemen a complimentary drink?" he asked.

The senior policeman nodded. "It's been a real tough night. We would much appreciate that, sir."

Back under the layers of colourful lights that blanketed the circular Kodak auditorium, the tight Estee Lauder Awards band played an extravagant musical sting. Branson was breathless with exaggerated delight, surrounded by the contestants, dancing a wee jig.

Flash moves completed, he gestured approvingly toward the band and the women and instantaneously there was appreciative applause.

"Ladies UND gentlemen," Branson crowed. "Without further ado, the winner of the 2009 Estee Lauder International Modelling Awards can finally be revealed. To assist me with the presentation, I am now joined by Giselle Richter, Chief Executive Officer of the Estee Lauder cosmetics corporation."

The crowd applauded the non-celebrity hesitantly. Richter arose from her front-row spot and swept up on stage - still in the jump suit and jacket that was now accessorised with a single large gold brooch.

As Giselle strutted her way up to the podium, Branson continued to meet his onerous contractual obligations.

"I must tell you that tonight's Awards would not have been possible without the generous support of the Estee Lauder cosmetics corporation."

The model contenders nervously contemplated the judges looming announcement. Well, almost everyone. Joanne winked cheekily at Angela who blushed and looked away.

Branson theatrically air-kissed The Gale on each cheek as she composed herself beside the podium. "Welcome Giselle," he said. But the M/C's body language was noticeably less relaxed.

Giselle offered camera 3 her best crocodile smile: all teeth, calculating eyes and rhinoceros thick-hide.

"Why thank you Branson, so nice to be here with you tonight."

"Giselle, I know that Estee Lauder's support for modelling talent around the world is greatly appreciated by all the girls," he replied with his best huckster's smile.

The producer cut to the models. The big screen showed camera 4's shot that passed along the line of contestants. All of them suddenly had forced professional smiles pasted upon their faces.

"I, like many others, have watched in amazement as these Awards have grown and grown over the past 10 years to become the biggest event in the global fashion calendar."

Giselle smiled and nodded as Branson continued ticking off the "specified key deliverables" she had personally written into the 2009 sponsorship agreement.

"On behalf of everyone who has been a part of this triumph since the beginning, on behalf of all the girls whose careers have been catapulted to Super Model status by these awards, I would sincerely like to thank Giselle and thank Estee Lauder."

Branson clapped both his hands above his head and forced his grin so wide he felt the makeup start to rub against his dehydrated skin. Leaving nothing to chance, the crowd controllers encouraged the audience to respond like they cared.

"Ladies UND gentlemen, I want y'all to give Giselle a great big warm LA welcome," Branson begged the audience. As the industry crowd applauded, Branson motioned for Giselle to move up the lectern.

She tapped the microphone with the nail of her left index finger. Two loud audio pops penetrated the packed auditorium. Branson nodded. The Gale frowned, unpacked a pocketful of notes, awkwardly perched a large pair of matron's spectacles upon her nose, cleared her throat and began.

"Good evening ladies and gentlemen. Estee Lauder is proud to have been the key strategic partner of these awards since the very beginning."

Branson nodded and theatrically raised the thumbs of both hands in front of his chest.

"Why are we here tonight?" asked the calculating executive. "Why have we facilitated these awards for 10 years? We're in the cosmetics business and we are very conscious of the power that models have over the minds of young consumer segments. We understand the key role models play in driving the purchasing behaviours of impressionable young girls."

"We're also aware of how difficult it is for emerging models to get their brands aligned with the integrated corporate architecture of the global fashion industry ..."

Three and a half minutes of dry corporate blah blah later and The Gale was still assaulting the ears of the audience with her droning, passionless voice.

Branson struggled to maintain his professional composure; while behind him camera 1 picked up Joanne and Miranda starting to fidget with their hands.

Giselle, oblivious to the negative body language screaming out of 3500 tormented souls right in front of her, ploughed on, ignoring her public relations manager's advice to keep the presentation short and sweet. She was determined to force every single one of her "key messages" down the throat of a huge global television audience.

"... So we intend to synergise the business drivers of these awards to leverage additional equity for our brand and create significant multiples of shareholder value," Giselle continued, explaining little in her colourless monotone.

An increasingly faint and disinterested audience response was accompanied by nervous looks from a growing number of models.

In the TV production suite, high above the stage, sat Johnny Morrison, a fat, bald, crinkle-faced cockney television event producer. Johnny was dressed in unwashed blue Armani jeans, a white John Paul Gaultier shirt, black Rick Owens leather jacket, black Dr Marten boots and he was wearing headphones and an accompanying hands-free microphone.

"Rotten" Johnny, as his sub contractors called him behind his back, was seriously losing his patience with Giselle.

"Fuck me drunk," Johnny muttered. "You might represent the principal sponsor, you fat fucking cow, but you're eating into network advertising time now. That's lousy fucking business on a good day."

And then, speaking directly at an image of one of the industry's most hated women mounted on a screen at the rear of the SSL C100 mix desk, he yelled: "You're costing us money. Worse than that you're messing with me and that's not just bad business, it's seriously fucking personal."

Johnny thumped the soft, padded end of his control desk, right behind the spare Terrapin FTR D6 video transmitter, clenched both fists and shook his hands in the air. The veins in his neck were bulging. He desperately needed to release the sense of frustrated rage that was growing inside him.

"Just fucking end it, you unprofessional pig," he screamed and pushed his chair back from the desk with his large boots. Johnny tilted his head back and rolled his blood-shot eyes toward the sound-proof panels on the roof.

But Giselle was not finished yet.

"Shut your trap, you sanctimonious fucking windbag or I swear I'll come down there and unplug your fucking microphone myself," Johnny started yelling once again, this time at the ceiling of the booth.

The Assistant Producer sent a message to Branson to shut Giselle up quickly or they would soon all be selling hotdogs for a living.

Down on the stage, Joanne's bored mind had drifted miles away from the suffocating cloud of management jargon. She was staring absent-mindedly at one Adam Verucce.

Adam, a plump bald middle-aged man, dressed in a crème linen Armani suit, was parked in the centre of the VIP front-row seats at the head of the catwalk.

Next to Adam sat two highly stylised blonde children. Adam appeared to be avoiding eye contact with Joanne. A blonde woman, clad in a grey hand woven tweed and braid Chanel suit, sitting next to the children, noticed Joanne staring at Adam. She turned her head and glared at the fashion designer, then swung her eyes back towards Joanne and frowned.

Joanne responded by smiling sweetly, she then fluttered her eyelids innocently and looked coyly at Branson.

Maybe Giselle was psychic? Maybe she felt the lofty producer's increasingly violent rage at her self-indulgent speech? Perhaps she had finally noticed Branson's cut cut cut hand signals? Who could know? Not one of Giselle's seven husbands had ever been able to stop her talking.

Mercifully for all in attendance, Giselle finally decided to call it a day.

"In closing, can I just say, Branson, that today, 10 years on, Estee Lauder still believes in the brand power and multi-platform functionality of these awards and it's a great pleasure to be here with you all tonight sharing the excitement, the fashion, the passion."

"Thank you Giselle," Branson said, jumping straight in. Calling on 15 years of experience hosting live television events, Branson instantly regained control of proceedings before the Harvard management school spawn could change her mind.

"Don't go away, we'll reveal who has won the 2009 Estee Lauder International Modelling Awards right after these important messages," Branson said, bringing his hands gently together and beaming into camera 1.

A musical sting went up and, on cue, the audience clapped - this time with relief.

Johnny sighed, pushed back in his chair and put his boots back up on the desk. His hands went up behind his head. "Thank fuck for that. You keep that cow on a leash now, Branson, she's had her 15 minutes of fame," he yelled into his headset.

"Evie, bring me some coke would you," Johnny continued. "Now would be good."

He paused and then responded to his assistant's query: "Yeah, yeah, a full one. Ta."

On the frontline, Branson moved up right next to Giselle at the podium and whispered to her. She shook her head and looked sternly at him through beady eyes. Her nose twitched indignantly.

There was an awkward pause as Branson waited for the commercials to finish and the telecast to recommence. Then, slipping back into showman mode, all silly grins and good humour, Branson, with a flourish, displayed a large pink envelope finished with a jet-black ribbon.

He gestured to the audience to be quiet. Branson repeated the shooshing actions to milk the moment.

"Ladies UND gentlemen, it's my great privilege to once again join with you and Giselle to discover who has won the Estee Lauder International Modelling Awards for 2009."

A hushed wave of anticipation fell upon the Kodak as Branson and Giselle leant forward at the lectern to open the envelope. After a brief cut with a pair of golden scissors, Branson lifted back the flap and Giselle pulled out the card. Her face became one big frown as she looked incredulously at the words in front of her. Branson leant in close and Giselle whispered in his ear. Branson nodded, took the card and fixed a tight polished professional smile upon his powdered face. Giselle, it would later be noted by FBI investigators, appeared less composed.

"Ladies UND gentlemen, for the first time in the history of these prestigious awards ..." Branson said and continued to stretch the moment.

The models, standing in a semi-circle looked twitchy. Well, everyone but the winners.

Angela, as usual, could not cope with her friend's mischievous assertiveness. So she tried to commit this winning moment to her memory, the spectacular auditorium, the adrenalin-charged atmosphere, the lights, the ecstatic capacity crowd, the photographers, the two gold statuettes twinkling on the lectern.

"We have two winners of the Estee Lauder International Modelling Awards," Branson announced dramatically.

The audience responded to the crowd controllers ordering them to gasp. Joanne looked up at the VIP boxes.

"The judges could not decide between a pair they described as two uniquely talented models," Branson continued.

Angela shook her head in faux disbelief.

Joanne was losing the struggle to hide a winner's grin.

Branson looked down at his card, slowly nodded his head and flashed his best huckster's smile.

"So the judges in their wisdom have decided that, in 2009, they are presenting both a catwalk award and ... a photographic award."

The Kodak screens featured another glimpse of the 12 models. Joanne brushed Angela's bottom with her left hand. Her friend looked down and gently shook her head while Miranda grinned expectantly at the pair.

"Ladies UND gentlemen, would you join with me in congratulating LA's Joanne Hart, winner of the catwalk category of the 2009 Estee Lauder International Modelling Awards," Branson finally announced and the band played funk.

Branson's hands and twisting and turning torso choreographed the wave of applause that swept the cavernous coliseum. Joanne appeared to be gasping for air.

Angela was so pleased for her friend. She genuinely could not stop smiling.

Giselle scowled and looked stone-faced at Branson. There would be words later.

Joanne stumbled forward from the pack, paused in front of Jenna Cheney and hugged her. Jenna recoiled from the embrace.

Joanne stood in front of her vanquished foe for just a second too long; an uber bitch in full flight. Then she turned on her elegant heels and strutted up to the podium.

"Joanne, our very own LA Super Model sensation, represents everything that is fun and sexy about fashion today," Branson declared, doing his best to ignore Giselle's profane glare. "We're on stage doing a live telecast for fuck's sake," he thought to himself.

"And Joanne was, I am told, a popular choice amongst the judges," Branson pattered on.

The broadcast pictures cut abruptly to the judging panel's first tier Kodak Presidential box where five extravagantly dressed fashion industry celebrities were pictured biting their lips, frowning into compact mirrors, rubbing noses, adjusting hats, pulling at ears, smoothing hair pieces and patting stomachs.

"No pretty pictures here folks, cut to camera 4," Johnny roared into his headset.

At the podium, Branson and Joanne embraced briefly before he ceremoniously presented her with a small gold statuette. With the lights shining off the symbol of her success, Joanne stared intently at the award as if she never expected to be holding such a precious thing.

The crowd's wave of applause pumped adrenaline through Joanne's body. Pure unadulterated joy surged through the world's most famous beach girl. Her detractors called it smug-satisfaction. Whatever it was, it was real and it was powerful and, at that moment, Joanne couldn't get enough of it.

Branson motioned for Joanne to move to his right, which she did.

Giselle stared meaningfully at Joanne, who returned the attention with her single most insincere smile of the day. They pretended to hug and, as they separated, air kissed. And then Joanne stood directly in front of Giselle and waved the precious trophy in her face.

Branson stole a wary glance at the card in his hand. "And Giselle, thank you, the winner of the 2009 Estee Lauder International Modelling Awards photographic category, all the way from Lyon, France, Ladies UND Gentlemen, it's Angela Durand!"

Branson lifted both his hands above his head and led the crowd's rousing applause.

Angela did her best to act genuinely shocked, as if the possibility of actually winning an award that night had never crossed her mind. She did the obligatory 'moment' commiserating with disappointed contestants - before ascending the podium to claim Super Model status.

But there was not enough karmic justice to go around in Los Angeles. The soon-to-be Super Model stumbled on the podium steps, fell forward and came to rest, awkwardly, upon her hands and knees.

Her dress had slid high, displaying acres of stockinged thigh and a lingering glimpse of the sheer black lace Aubade panties that partly covered her curvaceous derrière.

"Close up camera 2," Johnny barked into his microphone. "Camera 1, track in."

An electric jolt shot around the room. The fashion industry's next super-star lay there, prone and all alone, in full view of the world's cruel electronic eyes.

Giselle, wearing corporate composure like personal armour, quickly moved down the steps and carefully helped Angela to stand up.

"Are you OK Angela?" Branson asked, his voice laden with faux concern. "At last, we have a show," he thought to himself and just managed to check his inclination to grin.

Angela blushed and nodded as she straightened her frock. Branson and Joanne both sighed with relief. Giselle, who for half a minute looked like she cared, put her arm around the shoulder of the now thoroughly vulnerable and very human Super Model and escorted her up to the podium.

Every single feature written about Angela in every glossy magazine from *Vogue* to *Cosmopolitan* to *Hello* would, from that night on, run a picture of "the famous fall."

Ever the professional, Branson tried to ensure that Johnny and the broadcast crew had a more family-friendly picture for the telecast. He embraced Joanne and then walked her forward to the microphone.

"Joanne, congratulations," Branson purred. "You truly deserve this Award. How does it feel to be making a little bit of history tonight."

Joanne grabbed the microphone stand, rock-star style, with haste. She waved the statuette at the applauding crowd almost as if it was a weapon, certainly a vindication. Hundreds of flashes fired-off as photographers captured her immodest antics. She swivelled her svelte hips and gave every camera a turn at her best profile. Then she lowered the statuette to her side and almost swallowed the microphone.

"Thank you. I'm so shocked and surprised and happy, Branson, you just never think that this kinda thing happens to country girls," Joanne drawled and blinked.

There had been nothing else on her mind for weeks.

"I'd like to begin by thanking God for all her help, the sponsors for all their support, everyone at Estee Lauder, you've been brilliant, my mom, my step-father, my real father, Jesus, who is always with me, who has taught me to be kind and loving to everyone I meet, my twin brother and sister, my grandma - I really lurve you grandma," she said and a glisten crossed her already sparkling blue eyes.

"My grandpa - I really lurve you grandpappie, to my agent Reggie Sinatra, thank you, to my photographer Rainbow Heaven, everyone everywhere who has ever helped me. Thank you. You know who you are," she said, paused and smiled as she looked ecstatically around the Kodak.

"And to all of you, to the audience here in LA tonight, thank you so much, you guys rock. You're, like, totally awesome. You're the best audience I've ever had."

Then Joanne stepped back from the podium, raised the gold statue towards the audience with her left arm while blowing air kisses with the right, and beamed a 100 watt smile that could have been part of the global news cycle for a good 24 hours.

It was a sterling performance. Even Branson looked impressed.

Then Joanne raised her both arms - and the statuette - towards the ceiling, embracing the moment. The crowd loved the motion that liberated her pert left breast from inside the clingy crimson Alaia satin gown. If she had not been so totally focused on delivering her rehearsed performance she would have noticed the wardrobe malfunction that was about to become the defining image of her modelling career.

Just as the applause began to fade Joanne produced a handkerchief that, with her right hand, she used to dry her tearless eyes.

That brought them to their feet.

And then, barely breathing into the microphone, she said: "And to my dearest most beautiful friend Angela, Angela Durand, I am so proud to share this important moment in world history with you. So very proud! You should have won this award on your own, you are so-oh special."

Branson beamed at the blushing Angela and the screaming crowd sounded like they were demanding an encore at a Beatles concert.

"And Adam, Adam Verucce of Verucce Fashion Group, thank you Adam," Joanne continued breathlessly. "None of this would have been possible without you giving me my first little job all those years ago."

Out of all the thousands of people crammed into the Kodak, only Adam Verucce and Joanne knew exactly what sort of job she was talking about.

The crowd applauded as the pensive-looking Adam and his simmering-wife waved stiffly at camera 5 and received slaps on the back from surrounding admirers. Joanne was fluttering her eyelids so fast they look like blue butterflies on the wing.

"And to Brett, my darling, thank you! I love you so much babe. You are the sunshine of my life," she said sweetly and flashed her pearly white teeth at camera 2.

At that moment, someone pointed at Joanne's breast and a canny photographer, knowing a big money shot when she saw one, ignored accreditation protocol and started shooting flash clusters one after the other.

The smile vanished from Angela's face as she heard Brett Farrell's name. Giselle looked icily at Joanne and raised both eyebrows.

Mention of the footballer with a tarnished reputation had not been scripted.

Whatever he was, Brett was no country boy for a fresh-faced princess. "Joanne Says Super Star Romance Is Back On," ran one of the following day's *Gawker* headlines.

High above the playpen, looking down on Joanne's rock n roll antics, Johnny sat brooding amongst his control crew, equipment and a wall of 10 screens. As he looked directly at the screen in front of him, his eyes narrowed, he shook his head so hard his shoulder joints were cracking and the big bully slammed his right fist down on the control panel again.

"Branson, lose this dumb fucking tit-flasher immediately. Branson! Branson? You listening to me? Get her out of shot now. Now! NOW!"

Branson was fiddling with his earpiece. Joanne thought she saw some people sitting around Adam laughing at her. It was then, suddenly and to her horror, she realised that the end result of all that vigorous statuette waving had been a catastrophic wardrobe malfunction.

Her left breast and nipple was clearly visible, the firm tanned flesh stood out against the crimson fabric of the dress.

That breast she planned to keep for Angela, for after the after party, had stolen the show.

For just a moment, wolf whistles and bawdy laughter threatened to turn the awards presentation into a farce.

"Thank you so much Joanne and, again, congratulations," Branson said, his smile becoming broader and smarmier as he used his torso to block Joanne's bosom from the main camera shot.

"I don't care how hot she looks, pal, I am not broadcasting any more wardrobe malfunction shots OK," Johnny shouted at one of his young male camera operators as he grinned across the desk at a tense looking Assistant Producer.

Joanne quickly reinserted the attention-seeking breast into her gown with as much dignity as she could muster. But judging by the looks on faces in the audience - and the frenzied jostling of the paparazzi - there was not much dignity to be had at that moment. All her high hopes were suddenly in ashes because of some stupid sheer cut frock. Then again, they might not be talking about her wit, charm and intelligence across America tomorrow but they would be talking about her.

Simultaneously, as the confusion and embarrassment really hit Joanne, Branson proudly put his arm around Angela's shoulder and ushered her forward to the presentation zone.

"Angela, finally, here we are" Branson said, his arms spread and a smile as wide as the Mississippi lighting up his dial. It seemed like being close to such a beautiful woman had propelled him into a moment of Pentecostal rapture.

The ecstatic audience were on their feet as Branson handed Angela her statuette. Their unmistakable delight echoed around the Kodak dome for almost a minute until a grinning Angela brought her right index finger slowly up to her perfect lips.

While the crowd gradually resumed their seats, Angela blew a kiss to camera 3 and generously shared her billion dollar smile with the fashionistas in the house. Branson continued to highlight the girl from Lyon with his arms as she gazed at her award.

At that moment there was pure pandemonium in the Kodak Theatre, not a manufactured reaction. The fashion mafia and the cameras genuinely could not get enough of this petite French super star.

Joanne had to stifle a frown as it suddenly dawned on her that Angela was the obvious audience favourite and, with every step forward she took, Angela moved closer to becoming the centre of global attention.

"Angela congratulations on winning an Estee Lauder International Modelling Award, the most coveted award in world fashion. How does it feel right now?" Branson asked.

Angela's beautiful smile lit up the auditorium. Branson was still fiddling with his earpiece as she pressed her hands together, Buddhist-style, in front of her face and bowed her head ever so slightly.

"Oooooooohh, I'm so happy, and shocked, Branson. What an incredible audience you have here tonight. It's so very, very, humbling."

She had to patiently pause at the microphone as the thunderous crowd response threatened to lift the ornate curved roof right off the Kodak.

"I wish to thank everyone who has helped me over the years, especially my mama and papa and the Lord Buddha for making my world shine," Angela eventually continued.

"Can I just say to all the young girls watching tonight, dreams do come true, yes. You can turn your dreams into reality if you really want to. Just look at me. Anything is possible."

Branson smiled and told Angela to continue speaking over the riotous crowd as the telecast had to wrap in 60 seconds.

"A special thank you to my wonderful manager Reggie. To the sponsors, all my friends at Estee Lauder, to you Brad, mon ami, merci, and to all of you beautiful people in the audience here in LA, to everyone watching at home, thank you so much for helping to make my dream come true."

Angela slightly raised the statuette with her right hand, waved with her left, smiled happily at the animated audience and bowed fulsomely. Her long black hair cascaded forward and partially obscured the tears of excitement streaming down her face. There was nothing exposed to ruin this moment but she glanced down and checked her gown just to be sure.

Angela, Branson and Joanne embraced at the podium. The other 10 models looked on, some bearing thin disappointed smiles. Giselle tried to convey her personal disapproval but the wave of applause just kept on rolling through the theatre.

"Angela, Joanne I think the people have spoken," Branson said with a protective arm around both their shoulders. "Ladies UND gentlemen, another two stars are born here in LA tonight at the 2009 Estee Lauder International Modelling Awards."

Most of the extroverted Kodak people were on their feet as they launched into the night's final ovation.

"Thank you so much for being with us as we made history tonight," Branson crooned into camera 4.

"I look forward to seeing y'all again next year. Goodnight everyone."

Giselle deployed her best corporate crocodile smile as she watched over the happy waving trio and the crowd's umpteenth standing ovation.

It was a perfectly fitting conclusion to a TV ratings bonanza.

With 46 million *YouTube* viewers included, the telecast of the 2009 Estee Lauder International Modelling Awards was the second most watched American television event in history, according to the ratings agency Nielsen.

A couple of hours later and Joanne and Angela, dressed to thrill, were in their stretch limousine headed for *the* official Estee Lauder International Modelling Awards after-party.

Angela was smiling, Joanne scowling.

LA's favourite French belle wore a long black Chanel sheath dress and carried a black and white fringed tweed cravat jacket. Her classic outfit was accessorised with elbow-length black leather gloves, éternelle silver and pearl earrings, red Lancôme lipstick, red ballet shoes and the Chopard silver chain and peace sign prominent around her neck. Plonked down on the seat right next to Angela was a black Hermes Kelly bag.

The ultimate Californian beach babe shimmered like a vision in a lemon yellow Prada cocktail dress, black Agent Provocateur stockings and white Christian Louboutin skyscraper stilettos, accessorised with a silver Chopard bracelet and metallic lemon yellow Shiseido lipstick. A black Mulberry clutch bag sat by Joanne's left knee.

The jet-black limo was resplendent with uniformed driver, chrome and mirrors interior, a sleek black Baumatic fridge, B&W Zeppelin iPod dock, a cocktail blender, wine rack, glasses and a surprisingly large bench seat that Angela and Joanne were lounging upon.

Wilson Pickett's *In The Midnight Hour* filled their private pleasure dome.

"I'm gonna take you girl and hold you
And do all things I told you
In the midnight hour
Yes I am, yes I am."

"We've really made it now Joey, that's the only thing that matters," an adrenalin charged Angela cooed. Joanne knew her friend was right but the wardrobe malfunction had made her cross.

"These nobodies laughing at me has made me so, so, like, you know, mad! Tomorrow, there's going to be pictures of my tit everywhere. Tomorrow, no one will be talking about us winning Estee Lauders, they'll all be too busy staring at my tit."

"Vos beaux seins seront célèbres demain," Angela purred in reply.

"What did you say?" Joanne asked her charming friend with half a smile.

"I said your beautiful breast will be famous tomorrow, my friend."

The pair giggled liked children.

Angela warmed throatily to her theme: "Tes seins et mes fesses sont tous deux les célèbres."

"What the fuck are you on about French girl?" Joanne wondered jokingly.

"I said your breast and my bottom, they are both famous now."

Angela laughed soothingly and slid smoothly across the leather seat into Joanne's chuckles and open arms. She put an arm around Joanne's shoulder and tenderly stroked her mischievous breast.

Joanne sighed, relaxed and guided her friend's face in. They French-kissed passionately.

The Prince Regent Limousines driver watched through the rear vision mirror. It was beyond Martin's power not to watch. His eyes bulged in a voyeuristic kind of way.

Martin had already had a very long day. He'd picked up a corporate client at LAX airport at 7am and, since then, hadn't stopped chauffeuring people around the crowded streets and highways of the metropolis. Yes, he had felt tired and, yes, he had been dozing while waiting outside the Kodak Theatre for these spellbinding Model Citizens but his navy blue and gold embossed uniform was crisp and clean and his impressive peaked hat made him look like a handsome airline pilot.

With a can of Red Bull in his empty stomach and Angela and Joanne sitting behind him he really felt like a prince. A wave of both elation and longing swept through him. Eliza, his South Central sweetheart, would definitely not approve but the wild sexual energy swirling around these white girls was like nothing he had experienced before. He had felt more electric excitement in the few minutes since he'd ushered the two superstars of fashion into the back of his limo than in his whole lifetime.

Even though the job paid a lousy $12 an hour before tax, Martin was more than pleased he had decided to take the extra night shift.

At that moment in time he felt like he had been hypnotised, like he was under Angela and Joanne's spell.

Martin had entered a world so utterly different from the one he lived in, if he didn't have both hands busily guiding the steering wheel he would most definitely have pinched himself just to make sure he was not dreaming.

Like a fly on the wall, there he was, with a front row seat at what he was sure was the greatest show on earth.

Meanwhile, back in the model zone, Angela whispered in her lover's ear: "it is a great day for both of us, yes? Like you said, no more suits to please."

Joanne smiled warmly and nodded. Her delicious friend giggled and flashed that billion dollar smile. The last traces of Joanne's ego trauma vanished and the pair shifted even closer together on a seat the size of a queen-sized bed.

"Yes it is a great day for us, Ang, you are so right."

Joanne reached into her Mulberry clutch and pulled out a large plastic sandwich bag full of white powder. Angela slapped her right thigh with joyful abandon.

"It's party time Ang!" Joanne said as she dropped the bag onto the seat

"Oui, oui, and off to the soirée we go, mon amour," the delighted Angela replied and quickly folded her cravat before placing it under her bag.

A phone rang and Joanne frowned at her bag. "This had better be fucking important," she grumbled.

Joanne raised her eyebrows to Angela, extracted her iPhone and checked the caller ID. She sat up tall and turned the music up real loud before taking the call.

"Hello? Hello? Yes, what?" Joanne barked into the mobile. "Giselle? Oh yeah, Giselle, hi. Look I'm not sure why Reggie gave you this number but I can't meet with you next week. No, no, I'm on location in Europe."

She paused and listened, briefly. Her left hand stroked her blonde hair.

"What? Hello? Hello? Look, it's a terrible line and really loud where I am now. What? Look I can't hear you. Send me a text and I'll get Reggie to ... no, not tomorrow either. NO!"

For Angela's benefit, Joanne signalled with circular motions with her free hand that the caller was nuts. Martin glanced in the mirror and checked out the fast-moving scene behind him.

"Listen, Giselle, just text me! Yeah, yep, bye." And with that, Joanne abruptly hung-up and dropped the phone down onto the seat next to Angela. She took a deep breath, shook her head and made a deep guttural hissing noise.

"Was that Giselle?" Angela asked as she sat up straight on the bench and tried unsuccessfully to make eye contact with Joanne.

"Yes."

"Giselle from Estee Lauder?"

"Yes," replied Joanne who was still avoiding her friend's gaze. "What did she want?"

"Something about signing some paperwork. I can't believe she rang me directly tonight. I'll get Reggie onto it in the morning."

Angela stared at her friend quizzically. Joanne finally looked her in the eye and waved her away. "It's nothing. Just chop me a couple of lines will you Ang?"

Angela reached for the bag of white powder, the very best cocaine LA had to offer. Joanne's mobile honked as it received an SMS message. Angela picked up the phone to pass it over but Joanne, defensively, snatched it from her hand.

"Give me that," she snapped.

Joanne touched the screen three times. She stared thoughtfully at the message, pushed another button and held the iPhone up to her ear. At the same time, Angela started using her credit card to chop the Bolivian cocaine on a hand held mirror.

"Yes, yes, Giselle. OK ... OK. I'll get Reggie to talk to you tomorrow and make a date and time for us to meet soon," Joanne said flatly.

Angela's card temporarily stopped crunching into the mountain of powder as she gazed at Joanne, noting her increasingly tense body language.

"Hey, that's an outrageous thing to say," Joanne yelled into the phone. "If I hear that you've ever repeated that lie, you fucking pig, I'll have my Attorney sue you for every last dime you have. Just make sure you've got that real clear. Do you understand me?"

And with that, Joanne pressed the end call button without bothering to say goodbye and made a point of turning the phone off and throwing it back into her bag.

"Fuck I hate cells Ang, they're so, like, intrusive."

"Um, what's going on Joey? I knew there would be troubles, yes?" Angela said quietly with an anxious feeling spreading in the pit of her stomach.

"It's just about paperwork, believe me. That sour bitch is always looking for a fight."

Joanne slapped her right hand down onto the seat and shook her head. Angela was upset, her stomach started to churn. Joanne paused, took a deep breath, smiled gently at her friend and softened her tone.

"OK, I'll level with you Ang," she said as she reached out and stroked Angela's hair.

"Once upon a time I told that bitch she was the kind of corporate ball-breaker that turned men gay. And for some strange reason - maybe because it was the same day she discovered that her fifth husband had gone gay? - Richter has never forgiven me."

Joanne sniggered.

"Oh," said Angela, amused.

"It's her fucking problem, not mine," Joanne said sarcastically. "We won. She'll just have to suck it up."

"This is better than an episode of *The Young and the Restless*," Martin thought to himself as he gently slowed the limousine for a red light. He felt guilty listening in but he had a front row seat for the best soap opera he had come across in his 24 years on Earth and, like a suburban TV addict, he needed to know what happened next. Part of him was ashamed at what he was doing but he could not make himself turn off the back cabin emergency microphone.

As Martin accelerated the limo smoothly away from a busy intersection, Angela shook her right index finger back and forth in front of her friend's face. Joanne sighed, leaned over and kissed Angela full on the lips. She caressed her "bestie" tenderly and, suddenly without swagger, said quietly: "Don't sweat it French girl, our man Reggie will put the stone faced pig right back in her box."

Reggie Sinatra, the boss of LA's legendary modelling agency Model Citizens, was the personal manager of both women. Reggie was their number one 'fixer' of problems great and small. He would set things right, Angela knew that from personal experience.

Since the day two years earlier when, coincidentally, they had both signed up with the globally happening Model Citizens - since that happy day when Reggie had personally become Angela and Joanne's manager - the pair's career trajectories had been on a line going straight up.

One big break through had followed another. Long term contracts with the world's best-known fashion houses and unbelievable amounts of money were pouring in.

Beyond making beautiful business together, for the past 20 months, Angela and Reggie had been dancing along the edge in the lion's den of world fashion.

Gossip columnists, blogs and *Entertainment Tonight* had published and broadcast innuendo-laden pictures of the pair enjoying each other's company at gala events and nights on the town.

Angela had dreamt many a sweet dream about getting together with the charming, handsome and mysterious man from Model Citizens. However, because of the constant publicity and his ultimately introverted personality-type, they had never got beyond a very affectionate friendship.

No matter how many opportunities Angela had created for their relationship to move on up to the next level, Reggie had been determined to avoid the issue.

Or so it had seemed.

Now they had made it, Angela wondered, maybe, the time for hiding their feelings away had passed? She hoped so. The embers glowed red and hot between them.

Everyone around Angela and Reggie could see how comfortable they were together. Everyone who knew the pair thought they were made for each other. Their flirtatious adventures, their drunken evenings melting into each other's arms, had been over far too quickly for either of them.

Reggie could not handle being around when Angela was hanging out with one of her celebrity 'boyfriends.' She knew he had strong feelings too but ... he would not cross that line.

What was a girl to do?

With their busy interconnected schedules, between interviews and photo shoots and business meetings, it took far more energy and planning for Angela and Reggie not to just let their love flow.

They may have laid a golden commercial egg between them but theirs was as far removed from an ordinary business relationship as you could get.

A tangled ménage à trois had been built into the foundations of the rapidly growing Model Citizens modelling agency.

Angela knew she loved Reggie but she also adored Joanne. She had experienced girl on girl action and liked it. Whatever tomorrow might bring, Angela knew that right now when she and Joanne were together they could barely keep their hands off each other. And soon they were going to be sharing a house together. The 'do nothing' option was clearly not on the menu with her girlfriend.

While Angela struggled to comprehend her own aching desires for other members of team Model Citizens, Joanne had done some quick maintenance work: straightened her dress, checked her hair and quickly touched up her dazzling Shiseido lipstick, all with one hand as she held a chrome vanity mirror in the other.

U2's *Even Better Than The Real Thing* blasted through the limo.

"Give me one more chance
And you'll be satisfied
Give me two more chances
You won't be denied."

"Where are my lines, French girl?" Joanne asked as she finished her professional chores.

Angela lifted the mirror that carried four mountainous lines of white powder and a rolled 100 Euro banknote. She smiled sensually.

"Voilà. Ouais Joey, we're ready when you are."

Joanne pushed her vanity mirror away and turned side-on, pouting, to her friend. "How do I look girl?"

"Très bon, mon amour."

"What?" Joanne asked deadpan. "Why can't you jest speak American?"

"Er, you look great, my love, yes?"

Joanne smiled with satisfaction and stroked Angela's thigh before she picked up the rolled Euro note and greedily hovered up two lines of powder, one disappearing up each nostril. She placed the paper funnel back on the mirror, breathed deeply, sighed and hugged the air.

"Hmmmm, oh yeah, hmmmm," Joanne cooed and grinned. "I jest love this feeling."

As Angela picked up the rolled paper and proceeded to snort the remaining two lines, Joanne stroked her left thigh, nudging the Chanel dress further and higher up her leg.

Martin peeked in the mirror and liked what he saw.

"It's going to be a huge party, Ang," Joanne said. Her voice now sounded relaxed and dreamy. Every muscle in her body seemed to tingle with unlawful delight.

Angela smiled at her special friend as she delicately replaced the paper back on the mirror. A cloud of total euphoria descended on the pleasure dome.

"Yes, Joey, our grande soirée is going to be something really special."

Angela turned, picked up a magnum of Krug Clos d'Ambonnay 1995 champagne, popped the cork and sprayed some of the security screen separating the pair from Martin with the sweetest froth. She perfectly poured two flutes, handed one to her friend and lifted the other with her left hand.

Joanne was immobilised, staring at Angela with a fixed sensuous grin.

Angela was so happy. She was full of adrenalin and could feel the sexual energy pulsing out of her leggy girlfriend like a radiator.

The sense of anticipation was so delicious Angela wished she could just stop time forever at that precious moment. Push the pause button and live happily ever after, right there and then.

Martin was finding it almost impossible to concentrate on the road ahead. Every fibre of his being wanted to stop the limo and climb in the back.

"I would happily give up everything for one night with these femme fatales," he thought to himself as he ran a red light. A Los Angeles Police Department camera flashed but Martin really did not care that he had probably just forfeited his pay for the shift.

"Here's to us," said Angela and the pair in the back of the limo clinked glasses and drank.

"I kinda wish you were talking to me too," Martin thought to himself and smiled longingly.

"I can't believe how good you look girl," Joanne whispered, staring into Angela's shimmering brown eyes.

"Merci et saluer!" Angela replied, delirious with joy, as she lifted her glass and drank thirstily.

Joanne slid her right hand up Angela's dress, stroked her thighs and rubbed the front of her famous black lace knickers. Angela moaned and ever so slightly thrust her hips forward to meet her lover's caress.

The pair emptied their glasses and kissed again. The cocaine was pumping through their blood streams, heightening every sense and every incredible second of the hyper reality they had created.

Angela drew back from the kiss, beamed and then ducked in to nibble at Joanne's ear.

After a minute, Joanne leant back and then forward and Angela watched, fascinated, as Joanne slipped off her knickers and lightly caressed her private curves, her secret crevice. It felt so good. She was there, just momentarily, at the gateway to the palace of earthly pleasures before she walked right in.

Angela's inhibitions, her sense of reserve, her shyness, they melted away in the delicious white heat of the moment.

Angela leant forward and again nibbled at Joanne's left ear. Her talented tongue flicked at the lobe and teased the rim.

"Oh Ang," she moaned ecstatically. Angela closed her eyes and she filled her ear with warm air as Joanne expertly stroked her pleasure button. "I can't believe how good you look girl."

"You shine like a goddess. I jest can't take my eyes off you," Joanne whispered as she pressed her open lips to Angela's.

Angela opened her eyes and saw Joanne's beguiling mermaid's smile. Her blue eyes were ablaze with lustful joy.

Angela responded passionately with mouth and hands and felt an electric tingle rush through her as she stroked Joanne's perfect skin.

And so the floodgates were opened, their inhibitions finally thrown to the wind. Their hands were all over each other, reaching thirstily, as if they could never get enough. Angela rang her right index finger across the mirror, picking up what was left of the cocaine. She wiped it down the inner curve of Joanne's breasts; and then proceeded to lick the now infamous breast that, even as they relaxed into each other's arms, was being featured on hundreds of websites across America.

Martin loosened his belt and adjusted his pants downwards.

The women, at that exact moment in time the two most famous Super Models in the world, never even noticed.

After a kiss that seemed to go on forever Joanne bought the magnum of champagne to Angela's lips and encouraged her to drink. Greedily she took the head of the bottle in between her lips and let the sweet bubbly fluid slide down her throat.

"I dream about you, all day and all of the night, Ang," Joanne whispered into her ear as Angela surrendered herself to the many charms of her confident friend.

"Ooooooohh Joey," she replied as Joanne pushed her shoulders back against the seat, hitched her frock up high and poured champagne over her pussy ...

It was only later, much later, after the amorous pair had orgasmed, that they realised the limousine was no longer moving.

Martin had quietly pulled over into a Freeway rest stop. He sat there smiling boyishly, watching them through the mirror with that look in his eye.

"Hey, how about you get us to the show buddy," Joanne snapped into the intercom. Martin jumped to comply and, in his haste to compose himself, caught something sensitive in the zipper of his pants. The pain was excruciating. He yelped as his head hit the solid roof of the driver's cabin.

The pair giggled, but only for a second. Joanne popped the intercom on. "Are you alright?" she asked. "No," came his agonised gasp of a reply. The searing pain contorted his pretty-boy face. He whimpered.

"We had better take a look," said sensitive "nurse Angela" who opened the door, smoothed down her dress and, taking her lover by the hand, stepped out. "Please open your door," Joanne commanded Martin via the intercom before she followed her glowing Florence Nightingale on their urgent mission of mercy.

The next morning, at exactly 8.29AM, Angela was lying in bed with Gita, her purring silk-black Burmese cat, seriously hung-over but still resplendent in a black la Perla lace negligee. She was partially covered by a yellow camellia-print duvet and had a steaming cup of organic jasmine green tea in her hand.

Angela was half watching NBC's early news program on a wide screen TV.

Aretha Franklin's *I Never Loved A Man The Way I Love You* hummed away quietly in the background.

"You're no good heartbreaker
You're a liar and a cheat
And I don't know why
I let you do these things to me."

The weather report concluded with a storm warning. "More on that storm, and all the latest on the weather right across America, at the top of the hour. Des."

Angela had a vague recollection of the after party; of the pair of them arriving at the Vertigo Club, stepping out of the limo into a blast of cold night air and a huge wall of camera lights, leaving behind the happiest 'wounded' limo driver in LA.

She could remember one of the Awards telecast producers popping the cork off a bottle of Bollinger and then insisting the three of them hide in a cubicle and snort more cocaine. The quality was off the charts. She remembered that much.

Why the sultry Joanne had left the club so suddenly, right after Reggie's departure, she had no idea.

Angela's lazily ran her hands up and down the front of her body, caressing her soft olive skin, half asleep, dreaming of Joanne's talents and charms, just vaguely aware of the television's clichéd commentary that Gita's loud rhythmic purring almost covered over.

Then, all of a sudden, she was jolted fully awake.

"Jenny, thanks," said the program's male anchor. Des wore a gold slim-fitting Alexander McQueen jacket and matching shirt that touched off his dark hair and chiselled jaw.

"Now let's update the top news story we are following this morning: Brett Farrell, the troubled superstar of American Football, is in big trouble again," Des said sanctimoniously.

Both Angela's eyes popped wide open. She reached for her Sony remote and turned up the volume.

The TV pictures showed Brett charging down a football field, ball tucked under his left arm, brutally clearing multiple opponents from his path with his right fist and elbow.

"He just does not seem to learn, does he," added the show's female anchor Jenny, who wore a short grey Prada zipper dress and white blouse. She removed her horn-rimmed glasses with a disdainful flick of perfect blonde hair.

"And this time it's really serious trouble Brett has gotten himself into, according to our reporter on the scene, Felicity Robert," Des said matter-of-factly.

Felicity, a platinum blonde wearing a black Dolce & Gabbana pencil skirt and a black blouse with just enough silver adornment to let everyone know she was into the "bling thing", was pictured standing outside LA's Vertigo Nightclub. The vision cut back to Don, anxiously fiddling with his pen.

"Good morning Felicity, what has Mr Football done wrong this time?" he began.

Felicity rolled her eyes and displayed an NBC branded microphone.

"Good morning, Des. LAPD sources have told NBC that Brett Farrell broke the jaw of Lola Bellosace, the wife of convicted LA crime boss, Vince Bellosace, during a wild brawl outside the night club behind me during the early hours of this morning."

Angela shrieked and sprayed a mouthful of green tea over her duvet and poor Gita, who miaowed in protest and ran away. Angela threw the cup off the bed, pulled the duvet up around her body and hunched into foetal position, her tired eyes fixed on the screen.

In the television studio there was a stunned silence, followed by a sharp intake of air.

"I'm sorry. Can you run that by me one more time?" Des asked the reporter.

"Mr Football, Brett Farrell, broke the jaw of the wife of convicted LA crime boss, Vince Bellosace, during a fight earlier today," Felicity replied crisply.

"It's incredible news and hard to believe but a number of NBC's LAPD sources have confirmed the story, Des."

Felicity nodded to camera. Des sighed.

Tears began to well in Angela's sweet brown eyes. She wished more than anything that Joanne was laying beside her, the television was off and they were making jokes about famous tits and bums and bitching about the assets of other models.

"So how does one of America's all-time great footballers end up punching a woman in the face and breaking her jaw?" Des asked.

"Eye witnesses have told me that the Vertigo Club was hosting the Estee Lauder International Modelling Awards official after-party last night. Mr Farrell tried to force his way inside the club after security guards had denied him entry. The footballer is believed to have been inebriated. Drunk."

Co-anchor Jenny deliberately put her horn rimmed glasses back on, leant into the camera and asked in a serious tone: "What is it about the footballing culture of this country? What should be done about this kind of behaviour? What sort of role model for young men does this guy represent?"

"I just don't know. They are very serious questions you raise, Jenny. Troubling questions, without any clear answers," Des responded, trying to look as if he cared.

Alone in her giant bed, Angela moaned as *The Today Show* turned into her own private horror movie.

Where was Joanne? Was she all right? Had something terrible happened? Was she with Brett? Was she with someone else? My God, that coke. The Award's supplier had done them proud. Hadn't they decided they could be together now they were at the top of the tree?

"Why didn't we come home together?" she wondered.

"Models, eh?" the male anchor asked the reporter at the scene of the crime. Any thought of reforming the nation's football culture had already vanished from his shallow mind.

"Yes Des, models," Felicity replied and nodded, having worked with enough men in her lifetime to know exactly where their heads and hearts really lay.

"LAPD sources have told NBC that after Mr Farrell was refused entry to the popular A List night club, the footballer became aggressive and was involved in a scuffle with a number of Vertigo's security guards. The Bellosaces, who I understand were VIP guests at the event as long time sponsors of the Estee Lauder International Modelling Awards, just happened to be walking through the door when the confrontation became violent."

"An eye witness has told *The Today Show* that Mrs Bellosace's injury occurred when Mr Farrell threw a punch at a security guard who ducked and his punch connected with the side of Mrs Bellosace's head, knocking her down some steps and onto the sidewalk."

Angela had turned white. Both her fists were clenched tight. "Oh Joey, non, non," she cried out as Felicity continued reporting the appalling news.

She had never liked having to share Joanne with Brett, never. While the gossip magazines and blogs lapped up stories about the super-couple, "the Super Model and the Super Star of American football," Angela had been forced to remain silent and out of sight. She had hidden her feelings away but, after last night, she had thought to herself: "I am not going to be living in his shadow anymore."

"The Ronald Reagan UCLA Medical Centre has confirmed this morning that Mrs Bellosace was admitted a few hours ago and that she is receiving treatment for a broken jaw," Felicity continued dryly.

"A hospital spokeswoman described Mrs Bellosace's condition as stable."

"Do we know why Brett Farrell was trying to force his way into a modelling awards after party?" Des asked.

"Mr Farrell has been dating LA Super Model Joanne Hart, who last night was joint-winner of the prestigious 2009 Estee Lauder International Modelling Awards. Ms Hart was celebrating her victory at the club that Mr Farrell tried to force his way into."

As pictures of Joanne strutting a Milan catwalk filled her Sony TV screen, Angela was having trouble breathing. The ever-perceptive Gita jumped back onto the bed and Angela happily cradled the cat in her arms. The affectionate Burmese purred and licked and nuzzled her distressed mistress.

A picture of Joanne's smiling face continued to fill the screen, accompanied by the reporter's voice: "Despite the fact that Ms Hart recently told an LA gossip magazine they were taking some time-out from their relationship, it appears there is still a lot of feeling between the pair."

Angela's eyes went a puffy red as *The Today Show* broadcast pictures of America's favourite couple, Joanne and Brett, hand-in-hand outside a glamorous looking restaurant, on a float for St Patrick's Day celebrations in New York and celebrating another famous LA Eagles victory together on a confetti-strewn football field.

Angela shook her head and trembled. The pictures and words emitted by the TV were striking at her heart like knives.

The pictures of Brett and Joanne together ended abruptly, replaced by a close up of NBC's valley girl reporter Felicity.

"Friends of Ms Hart told me earlier this morning that she still loves Brett Farrell, despite his recent problems. The Today Show can confirm that

Joanne thanked him during an emotional speech she gave while accepting her Estee Lauder award last night. It would appear the super star love match is back on again."

Angela carefully lowered Gita into her lap, reached for her black Hermes Kelly bag and searched for her iPhone as *The Today Show* continued to robustly prosecute the case of the people versus Mr Football.

"A short time ago, Vince Bellosace spoke with journalists here in Los Angeles about the assault on his wife," Felicity added.

Angela, phone in hand, paused as pictures of a short fat man appeared on the screen.

The Don looked out through piercing dark eyes, his scarred face, puffy cheeks and pursed lips. He was the spitting sartorial image of an old school gangster in a sliver grey Zenga suit, white shirt and red silk tie. Standing at the branded lectern in one of the Hilton Universal's function rooms, Vince was surrounded by six physically imposing goons dressed in pressed grey pencil suits. One of them, bald, heavily tattooed and carrying a violin case, stood directly behind Vince.

"This footballer punk has got no respect at all," the Don said with feeling and crunched the lectern with his large right fist for emphasis. He paused and angrily shook the same clenched fist at the camera.

"After what he's done to my Lola, he's gonna wish he'd never been born!" the mafia man said loudly in a strangled tone.

Vince's goons remained expressionless.

The media pack yelled questions. In amongst the racket, an old-school *New York Post* reporter, resplendent in navy blue morning suit, porkpie hat,

Yankees tie and gruff Bronx accent, attracted his attention. Vince pointed at the scruffy hack.

"You, yeah you, you gotta question?"

"Have the police charged Brett Farrell with assaulting your wife?" the man from the Post asked.

Vince looked through the camera at the tabloid journalist and sneered.

"Not yet," he roared and thumped the lectern with his right fist again.

"How does that make you feel, Mr Bellosace?"

"What has happened to America?" the surly organised crime boss thundered. "It makes me wonder what kind of animal is allowed to behave in such a manner and go unpunished?"

Vince paused and reflected for a moment. He looked up, eyed the room and angrily shook his head.

Felicity leant forward in a fetching low cut plum red Prada gown and caught Vince's eye. He pointed directly at the blonde.

"Mr Bellosace, what would you like to say to Brett Farrell this morning?" she asked. In unison, the goons standing behind the Don stood taller and clenched their fists.

"Maybe the porca should be real careful when he crosses the road?" Bellosace muttered. "Maybe he should check his life insurance is paid? I think it may be possible that he could have an accident," Vince continued with thinly disguised rage in his voice.

"I don't know, I'm just a simple man who loves his wife and believes in justice."

The Don paused and took an extremely deep breath.

"Whatever happened to justice?" he asked indignantly and tugged at his jacket.

Vince finished right there. He stared through the large pack of media hyenas and made a Roman-style thumbs-down gesture with his massive right hand, as the crowd of journalists started to yell simultaneous questions.

But the Don had decided the show was over. He had sent his chilling message to Farrell.

"Let the pig sweat for a few days," Vince thought. Mission accomplished.

Two of the Don's goons stepped forward. One tried to put his left hand over the *Fox News* camera lens; while the other escorted Vince out of the room using a path the other four bodyguards had effectively bulldozed through the disorderly media circus with their elbows and palms.

Amongst the chaos of hard men loose around 100 squawking reporters and 50 television cameras, Felicity fluttered her eyes and passed the story back to the studio.

"It sounds like Mr Football has really crossed a red line this morning. Back to you, Des."

The Today Show host was sipping something from a large cup. His boyish grin showed he had been caught out.

Angel frantically dialled a phone number, waited and waited but got no answer.

"Where are you Joey?" Angela whispered to herself. Gita looked up and started gently kneading and purring, trying to please her usually carefree mistress.

Meanwhile, back on the small screen, back in the perfectly lit newsroom, Des lowered his expensive pen onto his executive clipboard and nodded an over-moisturised smile at his partner.

"You are so-oh right, Jenny, Brett Farrell just does not seem to learn. There are some days when you have to wonder if Mr Football is going to end up like OJ? What is his behaviour doing to the image of our favourite game?"

The blowhard talking head had never played a game of football in his life but, hey, that's infotainment.

Des nodded to the camera while behind him there appeared a large still picture of an angry Brett Farrell, wearing his LA Eagles football uniform, with fists held up in front of his chest in boxing style.

"We're trying to contact a spokesperson for Mr Farrell, for Estee Lauder, for the LA Eagles Football Club, but everybody seems to have gone to ground this morning."

He shook his head.

"It appears no one is available to answer our questions. What a disgraceful state of affairs."

Des paused and indignantly raised both his eyebrows to Jenny who frowned and, right on cue, shook her head.

"Are our footballers running out of control?" Des asked. "Our wonderful, inspirational NFL has built so many fabulous players, created so many heart warming stories of young men rising from the ghetto to stardom. Why should a few bad apples spoil the reputation of this proud American institution?"

Des frowned and shook his head.

"Please visit *The Today Show* blog and tell us what you think. Has the NFL completely lost the plot?"

Des scowled at the camera.

"Me, I want to know whatever happened to the good old days when footballers were our heroes and role models?"

Des and Jenny shrugged as one.

As the screen filled with images of Brett starring on the football field, Angela picked up the remote control, turned off the TV and, with tears again running down her face, she buried her head in her hands and sobbed like a baby. None of Gita's cutesy feline tricks could help.

After a long time weeping for her lost friend, Angela picked up the phone from the bedside table and again dialled Joanne's number.

Angela's calls were going unanswered because Joanne and Brett were still in a deep intoxicated sleep, covered by LovaSilk orange silk sheets, on a large four-poster bed in Brett's luxurious Mt Washington mansion.

The incessant ringing tone of Joanne's phone eventually awoke Brett. He turned on his side and revealed fresh bruises and finger marks on his arms and face, before rummaging in Joanne's Mulberry bag. Brett quickly pulled out her iPhone phone, glanced at the display, entered the owner's code, waved at the phone dismissively and turned it off.

"Bye bye, Angela," he muttered.

Brett stared at Joanne sleeping peacefully and sneered, sliding his hands under the sheets.

Joanne rolled instinctively toward Brett and cuddled up close to his broad athletic chest. She murmured affectionately and smiled in her sleep.

But this wasn't going to turn out to be such a warm, loving day.

Back in her bed, Angela yelled in frustration as the phone again clicked through to voicemail. Gita jumped up and ran under the bed. Angela touched the iPhone screen and, just as the fear started to rise, her phone played its distinctive Miles Davis tone. She jabbed her index finger at the screen and answered the call.

"Joey ... oh, Reggie, I was just about to ring you ... non, non, I don't know where she is."

Angela unburdened herself.

"I'm so frightened Reggie. Non, non, she's not answering my calls either."

She listened for 30 seconds, nodding her head as she cradled the phone to her left ear.

"Non, she left the Vertigo sometime around three. I'm not sure exactly when. Without saying a word, yes? Not long after you went home Reggie, she took a phone call, I saw that, and I don't know, she just disappeared after that."

Angela listened miserably, nodding her head.

"Please help me find her Reggie!" she whispered.

Fifteen minutes later and Angela - out of bed and wearing a Vivienne Westwood thing she used as a housecoat - was repeatedly dialling Joanne's number. She had made another cup of jasmine green tea, turned the TV back on without sound and, with a sense of morbid fascination, was again watching *The Today Show*'s smorgasbord of reporting on Brett Farrell: "the troubled genius of football."

A sucker for punishment, Angela grabbed the remote and turned up the sound. Guns and Roses *Welcome To The Jungle* accompanied the story:

"Welcome to the jungle
It gets worse here every day
Learn to live like an animal
In the jungle where we play."

The screen showed pictures of LA's favourite bad boy instigating on-field fights, scoring touchdowns, gambling, fighting, being photographed with glamorous women, shaking his LA Eagles captain violently by the jumper, setting up winning football plays and more fighting.

Angela listened to her phone but her eyes were glued to the super-sized Sony screen.

"Joey, where are you?" she said hesitantly into the phone. "Ring me. Please. As soon as you can."

As she spoke, pictures of an angry-looking Brett dragging Joanne by the arm from a stylish beach-front café filled the screen.

"Reggie is calling every 10 minutes wanting to book media interviews, wanting to know where you are?"

Angela stared bleakly at the old footage of Brett pushing Joanne into his rust gold Porsche 911 and slamming the door shut, punching a television camera operator in the side of the head and then yelling at other reporters before he jumped into the car.

Joanne was wearing a strange half-smile on her face and, just for one moment, looked as if she was enjoying herself. Brett started the car and accelerated straight at a scattering media pack which, just this once, was not going to stand its ground. As the Porsche raced away, the footballer's left hand appeared through the window and offered the cowering journalists a one-finger salute.

"You better not be with 'eem, Joey," Angela said pointlessly. She knew intuitively that the worst-case scenario was happening. Again.

Later that morning, Joanne lay hand-cuffed to Brett's bed. Illuminated by candles and spotlights, Joanne had been tied face-down to the huge 4 poster.

She was dressed in a dark Assia vinyl lingerie mini dress, pink suspenders and a pink crotchless thong, finished with pink fishnet stockings, pink Shiseido lipstick, and a pink cashmere béret. Joanne's heart pounded and her eyes blinked nervously as Brett loomed large behind her in a black one-piece spandex body suit.

A childish smirk possessed the front of Brett's battered head. A large ink-coloured bruise surrounded his swollen left eye.

Joanne's legs were spread and restrained by two red Burberry silk ties attached to the bed-posts. Her handcuffed hands were tied with rope to her torso. Brett stared admiringly at his handiwork, then reached to one side of the bed and pressed a button. Joy Division's *Love Will Tear Us Apart* suddenly erupted from six massive Bang and Olufsen speakers around the room.

"Why is the bedroom so cold?
Turned away on your side
Is my timing that flawed?
Our respect run so dry?"

Joanne heard the song's maudlin lyrics like she was in a dream. In just a few days time, she would wish she had paid a lot more attention.

Choosing from an assortment of bondage toys he had laid out on a butcher's table by the other side of the bed, Brett picked up a heavy leather whip lifted up Joanne's skirt, tugged her thong down just below her gym-toned cheeks and brought the whip down hard.

She yelped as the lash burnt her skin and sent a shock of searing pain racing up her spine.

"Repeat after me slut, I am a naughty girl," Brett told her menacingly as he brought the whip down twice.

As he inspected the three crimson straight lines that now adorned her taught pale skin, Joanne responded obediently.

"I am a naughty girl."

"What else do you need to tell your master?" he asked and hit her with the whip again. Joanne yelped, arched her back and clenched her fists helplessly.

"I have been a very naughty girl, I have misbehaved sir."

Brett leant forward and pinched her left nipple as he whispered coldly into her left ear.

"And?"

"And I need to be punished sir," Joanne replied in the breathy little girl's voice she knew he liked.

Brett unleashed a flurry of blows with the whip. "No, no, please sir, no," Joanne wiggled her bottom as she pleaded. Brett paused and leaned in close to her face and she smiled submissively.

"Now say it like you mean it," he growled contemptuously.

"I have been a naughty girl, master. I have misbehaved and I need to be punished. Please punish me sir."

Brett smirked, picked up a small black remote control, pressed a button and a red flickering light appeared on the back of the camera mounted at the end of his bed. Brett proceeded to whip Joanne rhythmically. She cried out as lines of purple and red appeared on her bottom. The pace and intensity of the lashing increased and moved up her back. She started to scream and the muscles visible in her toned body convulsed.

After landing more than 20 cruel blows, Brett stopped and, for a moment, stroked her tense face.

"Oh, dear, oh dear. What have we here?" Brett asked mockingly as he fingered and poked a dozen swollen weals with his right index finger. "You are looking a little red-assed now slut."

"Hey, no marks, please sir, no marks, you said no marks sir," Joanne begged.

"Hey, that's what happens to bad girls," he said and laughed cruelly. "You should know that by now Joey." Brett nodded and again stroked her face tenderly for just a moment. He placed the whip down on the table but immediately picked up a cane and a paddle shaped like a table tennis bat and alternately stroked and spanked her sore derrière.

"Please stop, that hurts," she begged. Brett threw the paddle down on the bed beside her face and roared at her from up close. "Be quiet. Ask your master to service you."

"Please use me to come sir. Please let me service you master. Please use me to come. Purlease," she whimpered.

Brett frowned and shook his swollen, unshaven head. "No" he said and slapped the right side of her face and then picked up a large red ball gag and forced it into Joanne's mouth.

"Open it, open your mouth," he commanded and she did as she was told.

"You know I don't expect to have to tell you things twice," he told her coldly. Joanne felt a chill run down her immobilised spine and noticed that strange, dark, addictive energy was rising within.

He spanked her twice more. The stinging pain and the dull throbbing sensation of the weals Joanne could feel flipped her mind and turned her on. She felt her juices flow and, uninvited, a wide submissive grin formed upon her face.

Brett felt a triumphant hedonistic rush as he forced the gag deep into her mouth. "That's better, much better," he said matter-of-factly.

He slapped Joanne's face again, pinched and roughly pulled at her right nipple. She gasped in pain and with excitement as he wrapped a huge right hand tightly around her throat. Her eyes grew big as she struggled to breath. He leaned slowly forward from the hips until his face hovered close to hers.

"You ever talk about leaving me again and I'll be selling your bondage films to the Internet guys," he threatened and paused for maximum effect.

He brought the cane down twice more and she wailed and she moaned. "They'll be hot for your tushy. I'm sure the San Fernando boys will pay big bucks for porn starring a big name celebrity slut like you," he growled.

Joanne nodded her head, frightened, confused, overwhelmed by adrenalin, pain and excitement. Why did it have to be like this?

"Why can't he be loving, like he sometimes was," she wondered. "Why do I get off on being treated like this? Pleasure from pain? What's wrong with me? Why can't we be normal? Does he love me?"

Her drama loving, exploited, manipulated and over-stimulated mind went round and round in circles. Again.

"There must be something wrong with me," she thought.

She tried so hard to break free from her bonds, to scream no, but her restraints held tight. She was stuck like a fly in a spider's web, her voice and words muffled by the gag. Her personality submerged and drowning. Her tears turned into a flood and jet-black mascara ran untidily down both Joanne's cheeks.

Brett laughed scornfully as he rummaged around on the table and picked up a heavier cane.

"It's just like those early humiliating fashion castings you used to do," the little voice inside told Joanne reassuringly. "Submit. Give him what he wants and eventually you'll get what you want." Brett waved the cane up and down beside her face. It cut through the air with an intimidating swooshing sound.

"Hey, you should try being a little more open minded Joey. You should know porn will be good for your career, slut, because your master is telling you it will be," he said in an obnoxious tone.

She nodded helplessly and Brett gave her bottom more cutting strokes. Joanne wriggled her helpless derrière as the cane rained painfully down upon her. Soon another dozen dark crimson lines stretched across her cheeks and a few droplets of blood glistened in the fleshy canyons he had created. Her wrists and ankles jerked instinctively, against her cruelly tight restraints.

As Joanne tried to block out the savage onslaught by dreaming of his large and talented cock, Brett suddenly flicked her béret off and pulled a pair of black blindfold glasses down over her eyes. She tried to make her muffled complaints heard but Brett just laughed out loud and brought the cane down again.

"Just be quiet and pay attention to your master," he yelled at her. She nodded and tried to smile reassuringly through the gag. "If you ever tell Angelina, or Reggie, or anyone else, about the tapes, I will sell them to one of the porn networks, OK? Do you understand me?"

Joanne nodded her head. Brett removed the blindfold and leant his head in so close that the spider and the fly were literally eyeball-to-eyeball. He again gripped her throat tightly with his right hand.

"I do hope you got me Joey," he said quietly as he roughly pinched and pulled at her left nipple with the fingers of his left hand. She shuddered with pain and again felt completely overwhelmed by fear and dark desires.

"Don't forget now, slut, because I ain't going to warn you about your behaviour again. Do you understand me?" he demanded to know as his empty eyes tore into hers.

She nodded energetically and repeatedly shouted "thank you sir" through the gag as the heady mix of adrenalin and survival instincts overrode her conscious being. Her hands opened and closed as Brett took her nose between the thumb and forefinger of his right hand and slowly pinch-closed both her nostrils.

"How would your step daddy handle knowing what a whore slut his widdle princess really is?" Brett asked and slapped her horrified face. "You know he's always so-oh wanting to be photographed with me at sports functions, don't you?"

Joanne winced and whimpered, her pretty features creased as the river of tears tried to wash her mascara-stained facial skin clean.

"Not so tough now, are you?" Brett asked and Joanne immediately shook her head.

He stroked the flesh of her left foot with the cane and then abruptly dropped it onto the floor and walked menacingly back to the head of the bed. He clicked the iPod and started humming along as Brett and Joanne's theme song repeated.

"And lurve, lurve will tear us apart, again," he croaked tunelessly.

Brett replaced the blindfold over Joanne's terrified eyes and ignored her muffled pleas for mercy. He laughed unkindly, picked up the heavy whip again and struck at the vulnerable flesh on her back and lower thighs.

But Joanne knew from experience that her punishment was nearly over and soon his attention would switch to sexual conquest.

Sure enough, after three blows, the whipping stopped. Brett unzipped his leather trousers, tore the remnants of her thong off with his primitive hands and, with a single brutal stroke, penetrated her ass.

Joanne screamed as loudly as she could, like her life depended upon it, but in that burning moment of torment and despair, nobody but the love of her life could hear her desperate cries for help.

Simultaneously, miles away, in the concrete canyons downtown, Giselle Richter was in her spacious high-rise office. She sat at her huge desk, wearing a black Yves Saint Laurent pantsuit, sipping an extra-large Starbucks coffee and ignoring the panoramic LA city views from her window that crystal clear morning.

The Gale was laughing hysterically at a large picture of Joanne's wardrobe malfunction, under the headline Super Model Hangs Out In LA, on the front page of The *LA Daily News* lying upon her desk.

"I'm going to get this framed," she told herself in a cheerful voice.

The following evening, the claret-coloured sun set blazingly outside the fashionably minimalist offices of the Model Citizens Inc Modelling Agency on Mateo Street in LA's bohemian Arts District.

The Model Citizens office function area was standing room only, packed with loud beautiful people and heavyweight fashionistas.

The room was a smorgasbord of colourful new season's haute couture creations - Chanel, Louis Vuitton, Armani, Dior, Dolce & Gabbana, Givenchy, Gucci, Prada, Yves Saint Laurent, Versace - dazzling white teeth and perfect hair.

At the back of the room a line of serious looking cameras were perched on top of elevated tripods.

There was a restless, extroverted, conversational buzz in the air. On stage, a young DJ was making her final preparations at three turntables to launch happening vinyl sounds into the room.

Dozens of posters of models, their gold-framed photographic composites, and classic black and white fashion advertisements dominated the walls of the room. Caterers, dressed in white uniforms, ferried food and drinks on silver trays.

The colourful crowd - models and their lovers, agents, designers, photographers, rag trade entrepreneurs, celebrity fashionistas of every kind, publicists, bloggers, agency staff and assorted hangers-on - chatted over the top of a house music compilation.

The sense of expectation in the room, reflected by the volume emitted by the crowd, just built and built. Reggie's choreography was just right. After a few more minutes, he rang an old ship's bell five times. The lights dimmed. Angela and Joanne triumphantly entered the room for the "impromptu" celebration drinks Reggie had organised.

Shining in the spotlights, the pair made a grand entrance, arms entwined, to loud and rapturous applause. This was the first big party after the after party and the world's latest Super Models were determined to celebrate their Estee Lauder triumph with a couple of hundred "close personal friends."

Joanne brought to life a tight blue Mouret cocktail dress, shiny yellow Dr Marten lace-up boots and carried a black Burberry bag.

Angela shone in a vintage Balenciaga cocktail dress that silhouetted black lace floral motifs over deep red silk, a red woollen béret and flat red Gucci ankle strapped sandals.

The cameras feasted on the glamorous pair, focused on every fabulous skin pore as they air-kissed their way through the room and schmoozed. Fleetingly.

The hottest names in fashion were repeatedly embraced with varying levels of good will. The super stars of Model Citizens Inc were in da house!

Joanne moved to the corner, by the impressive boardroom door, and hugged and kissed two footballer types, squeaky clean in matching sharp, dark Prada suits and shiny Duckie Brown shoes.

"Isn't it fabulous?" she asked them in an excited tone. The boys nodded in agreement as Joanne slipped an arm around each of their waists.

The envy of everyone; she was thrilled knowing every single move she made was being closely watched. In the middle of the crowd stood Jenna Cheney. Dressed in an old black denim Dolce & Gabbana mini skirt and laddered black stockings that were oddly matched with a formal white Ralph Lauren business shirt and red pumps, Jenna was in another world, deep in a conspiratorial conversation about Joanne's wardrobe malfunction with another anorexic blonde in a crème mini skirt, matching Gucci t shirt and maxi black heels.

Nearby, Angela was in a relaxed conversation with an impeccably groomed 40-something woman in a Givenchy black Twedo pantsuit and blue low-heeled Manolo shoes.

"Thank you so much Nellie. Your support has always meant so much to me," she cooed and kissed her friend lightly on each cheek.

After watching the slowly relaxing party girls like a proud parent, Reggie Sinatra moved to interrupt and shepherd Angela and Joanne towards the Board Room door.

Reggie wore a beautifully cut black Armani single-breasted suit, no tie, set off by a loud saffron Pierre Cardin shirt and black Birkenstock Memphis shoes.

A blue-eyed 36-year-old Brit who had lived in LA for 10 years, Reggie still spoke with a trace of London in his voice. He stood 6 feet 2 inches tall, with the high posture and taught-sinewy build you would expect from someone with a black belt in Yoseikan-Budo Karate.

A master of people skills, Reggie sensed that Joanne had some kind of friendship and favour agenda with the two male models. He smiled agreeably at both of them as he placed an arm around Joanne's shoulder and nodded at the door.

"Sorry to interrupt you guys. She'll be back in 20 minutes, I promise."

Joanne smiled sweetly at the pair and gave their butts a quick squeeze. Reggie placed his right hand gently on the small of her back and guided his prized client forward while his left hand swung open the boardroom door.

"If I miss you later, Marc, do text me at six on Friday," Joanne said. "Don't forget darling!"

Marc furtively took Joanne's hand and kissed it. "Enchanté" he said with feeling and smiled longingly at her.

Joanne grinned playfully at the boy and slowly retracted her hand.

Reggie waltzed her inside and gently closed the Boardroom door.

Inside the sound proofed room Reggie was, on the surface at least, very happy as he locked the door. A wide grin spread across his chiselled features. He gestured for Angela and Joanne to sit on the world's funkiest black Fritz Hanson couch, placed to the left of a splendid Stormy Oak board table, 12 ergonomically-correct executive chairs, black drawn curtains and a sparkly polished mahogany floor.

Reggie remained standing and paced slowly up and down the room, past the framed pictures of the Agencies' top six models. Angela removed her béret, shook out her hair and smoothed it with both hands.

"You know, you guys are number one on our books now," Reggie said with a chuckle. "Joint number ones, because we don't want any status squabbling among friends do we?" he joked and lightly touched the shoulders of both his Super Models.

"Squabble? Us?" Joanne asked Reggie with mock indignation.

Angela threw an arm around Joanne's shoulder "Liberty! Equality! Fraternity!" she declared and giggled.

"There will be trouble if she keeps coming out with all this revolutionary French political crap Reggie," Joanne teased and gently poked her left index finger into Angela's stomach. "We're rich now girlfriend, it's time for you to move on up."

Angela smiled patiently at her Californian friend, shook her head and brushed Joanne's hand aside. "Buddha said to grow tall, a tree needs deep roots," she replied serenely.

Joanne threw both her hands up in the air. "OK, OK. I surrender, Marie Antoinette, please have mercy on me."

"Speaking of la belle France," Reggie continued as he moved to the polished steel bar cabinet in the opposite corner of the room. He opened the fridge, flourished a chilled bottle of Perrier-Jouet champagne, popped the cork and carefully poured three glasses from the magnum.

"Now you're talking Reggie," Joanne enthused.

For just a moment, muffled crowd noise followed by raucous laughter seeped through the wall into the room as the DJ began her set and the party outside stepped up a gear.

"Have I told you how proud I am of you guys?" Reggie asked. "We really showed the weak hearts, the cynics, the disbelievers, didn't we?"

Reggie gently stroked the girls' shoulders with his hands. His smile was a mile-wide; it was clear there would be none of his characteristic cynicism today. Angela and Joanne were happy to soak up the flattery. Reggie handed both of them a serious glass of champagne.

"Merci, Reggie," Angela said and sipped her over sized bubbly.

"You have both made me a very happy man," Reggie declared.

"Ooooooohhh, this is good champagne," Angela replied and took another large sip. "It's Perrier-Jouet," Reggie replied and drank.

"Très bon," Joanne told Angela and giggled. "See, I am learning from you French girl," she said and tasted the premium champagne.

Angela and Reggie laughed. Joanne smiled affectionately at the pair as the trio emptied their glasses.

"Why thank you, Reg," Joanne joked as he refilled the flutes.

Reggie raised both his hands level with his shoulders, palms facing each other. "You two can call me Reg, you can call me anything you like, just as long as it's me you are calling, yeah."

Reggie laughed deep and long and Angela and Joanne happily shared the up vibe. He encouraged the pair to stand and come together for a group hug.

Mission accomplished, they sat together on the long and comfortable low-level couch and drank. Reggie refilled the three glasses in turn and they shared some more fraternal laughter and light-hearted fashion gossip.

Next thing, Angela and Reggie were holding hands. Again.

"Isn't this fun?" Joanne asked. "It's party time guys! It's our time in the sun!"

She put her hands on the couple's shoulders. "Maybe it's finally your time too, Reggie? Ang? Like, you guys are such naturals. What do you think?"

Reggie squeezed Angela's hand tight and kissed her lightly on the lips. Angela could not help but wonder if Joanne was trying to palm her off. "Maybe I'm not good enough for you sexually?" she thought.

And Reggie? Reggie stayed on message. It was business first, second and third.

"What do I think? Well, this morning I woke up thinking of just how far the three of us have come in just two years."

"It's amazing," Joanne agreed.

The three musketeers saluted, clinked glasses, smiled at each other and hedonistically drank with their arms entwined as one.

"I would like to take a little time out right now, kick back and party," Reggie said. "But our currently huge window of opportunity will not last long. Monetising the Estee Lauders breakthrough is the agency's priority. I can make both of you an additional 20 million on the back of these awards before the end of the year. At least 20 mill, possibly more."

Angela and Joanne gasped and exchanged high-fives.

"20 million, here's to it," Joanne declared and rubbed her hands together. She grabbed her glass and rapidly emptied it.

Reggie also looked pleased with himself. In the past two years he had invested a lot - financially and emotionally - in this pair of freshly minted Super Models. Their return on investment had already cleared all of the agency's debts and that was before the Estee Lauder Awards, a night of nights as far as cash flow was concerned.

After winning the awards, the coming year of commission income from Angela and Joanne's beautiful career trajectories promised to set Reggie up for life.

Better still, he might have had a really comfortable working relationship with Joanne - and their overt displays of friendship at the numerous functions they attended together were only half faked - but he was coming to realise how profoundly he loved Angela and the feeling was obviously mutual. What could be better?

"Of course it does mean more travel for both of you," Reggie continued faux casually. "A lot more time working in Tokyo, London, Paris and New York. What do you think? Are you up for it?"

"Reggie, I think this sounds too good to be true," Angela said and unleashed her vintage heart-melting smile.

"Hey! Just remember all the bad times," Reggie replied. "You guys have worked so damn hard to create this moment. You really deserve everything success has to offer. Both of you."

Angela and Reggie hugged each other tightly. "You guys are kindred spirits, living in denial," Joanne thought to herself in a rare reflective moment.

"You do know almost everyone who sees the body language of you two together assumes you are an item, a happily married couple. You do know that, don't you?" Joanne asked the soul mates quietly. Angela took Reggie by the hand and gazed into his sparkling eyes.

While Reggie thought of himself as a thoroughly modern man, much of his personality had been shaped by emotionally unavailable parents and the buttoned-up English boarding school they had sent him to when he was just nine years old. Then there were the five long lonely years he had spent consuming law books in Oxford University's Bodleian library.

Whatever his self-image, the reality was that Reggie was another charming, intelligent and emotionally barren product of the British establishment. Born and bred to deploy a stiff upper lip, he would rather run across one hundred lanes of peak-hour freeway traffic than take a risk with his feelings.

That's why Reggie, once again, reflexively chose to avoid the quick sands of his heart. He changed the subject. He dropped Angela's hand and jumped to his feet. Flipped up a silver lid sitting on a white portable workstation and turned on his MacBook Pro laptop. "OK, lets get down to business guys," he declared, suddenly officious.

Joanne looked quizzically at Angela who, having watched this behaviour repeat and repeat, shrugged her shoulders nonchalantly. She turned, a little hurt, to look at the big red door and longed to escape Joanne and Reggie's rejection by immersing herself in the party now noisily in full swing just meters away.

Reggie opened a PowerPoint presentation on the computer, clicked on the first slide and cleared his throat.

"To fully monetise your Estee Lauder potential, we're going to solidify your Super Model brand status in the next two months," he announced and Joanne nodded.

"Beyond scheduled modelling assignments, you guys will be doing an exclusive 'friendly' interview with Hannah; pitching for voice-over work for the next Disney cartoon, shooting new multi media portfolios and accepting Ambassadorial roles for *Greenpeace*, *Save The Children* and such like."

Reggie spoke to the slides in that measured formal English tone he prided himself on being able to deliver when under pressure.

"We need to do Hannah in the next few days, while the brand perceptions are still positive. While everyone still remembers the fact that you two became Super Models the night you won the Estee Lauders."

He stood facing the pair on the couch, sensing their distraction, their real desire to join the partying throng.

"But, like, we are moving into the Venice investment house in a few days time Reggie," Joanne protested.

"And I have an 'ot date in New York, oui?"Angela added as she reengaged in the discussion with some payback.

Joanne looked mildly surprised.

"Awesome news, girlfriend. Is it Brad? We all know how hard you have sweated on that one," she gushed.

Reggie's heart sank. Angela coyly sipped more champagne and looked up at the roof. "Well that might be considered telling, yes," she said rather quietly.

Reggie looked and felt more than a little deflated at this news but his little voice inside was telling him "see this is why you don't mix work and pleasure." He stared straight ahead, projected an emotionless face and focused on the task at hand: the business interests of Model Citizens Inc.

Joanne poured herself more champagne but as she moved to refill Reggie's glass he put his hand over it and ever so slightly shook his head. "I've got meetings later," he explained. Angela waved away a refill as she took another sip from her glass.

"C'mon Ang! Give it up girl. Of all the people you've pulled? How can you keep quiet about him? You are full of surprises, French girl," Joanne loudly teased and taunted the odd couple she shared the room with.

Angela just smiled an enigmatic Parisian smile and looked once more toward the door. Reggie felt a horrible sinking feeling deep inside but cleared his throat, fiddled with the computer, and clicked on to the next PowerPoint slide.

"Let's book Hannah for Tuesday, I have already spoken to her people and we're good to go, they've pencilled us in. Tuesday gives us time to do a couple of practice interviews with my producer friend, Grant."

Reggie clicked the computer and brought up a flow chart.

Joanne was shrugging to concentrate, both hung-over and still stoned from the previous night. A sharp pain lingered in her intestinal regions. The whipped skin on her bottom was so sore that even the soft leather caress of the couch was painful. So she looked at the roof, glanced at her colleagues and friends, fidgeted with her hands and rearranged her legs.

Angela was faraway, too, her hands in her lap, her brown eyes vacant, her demeanour a little on the sad side.

Reggie knew from experience he had a maximum of 10 minutes to close the deal and save Joanne's career. So he threw caution to the wind and seized the moment.

"Look forget about the move, would you," he said in a tense aggressive tone that Angela and Joanne rarely heard. "My people will set up the house for you. They'll do everything."

"What's important right now is taking control of your image. We have to be out there in the market place in damage control mode, protecting brand Joanne, because Farrell took most of the shine off your win."

Joanne frowned and looked at her feet but Angela was suddenly all ears.

"Do you understand how much damage he's doing to you professionally Joey? Do you?" Reggie asked empathetically and stared at her but Joanne was determined to avoid eye contact, moving her sore bottom around on the couch, unable to settle. Reggie pressed on.

"You guys should be signing multi-million dollar contracts and going on holidays. Instead, brand Joanne is covered in mud. The Estee Lauder people are seriously unhappy, as you know Joey ... I'll tell you again, we should be putting as much distance between you and Farrell as possible."

Angela looked at Joanne and nodded in agreement.

"I don't want that psycho intruding on my image-control-strategy again. Ever! I'm well over it Joey. This is the third time in a year that he has cost us millions."

Joanne cast a sulky glance in Reggie's direction. She wrapped her arms around her waist. Reggie noticed the wall going up but he was determined to crash through.

It was now or never and he knew it.

"What's the solution?" he asked Joanne preemptively. "You play the victim, you walk away and we turn the whole fucking debacle to your advantage."

Both Angela and Reggie were trying to make eye contact but Joanne kept her stare down on the floor as a kaleidoscope of contradictory thoughts and images swirled through her tired, overloaded and suddenly grumpy mind.

"I don't give a fuck about what happens to that sick piece of shit. But your fling thing with that loser has got to end and end now, Joanne, or you will end up on the receiving end of a mafia hit too. Do you understand me?"

Still Joanne looked down at her Dr Martens and when Angela reached for her friend's hand, Joanne dismissively slapped her fraternal gesture away.

"Do you understand me Joanne?" Reggie growled, deploying a venomous tone his super star clients had never heard before. He thumped the workstation with a karate chop and knocked over his glass of champagne.

As Reggie worked hurriedly to rescue his laptop and other gadgets from an advancing sea of bubbly white fluid, Joanne reacted indignantly.

"But I might not want to abandon Brett. It's my life. He might be the one for me, who are you to say? What do you know? Either of you?" Joanne's voice was cracking as she replied.

Truth be told, she wasn't sure what she thought about Brett and his violent psychopathic ways. But her instinctive response was to stand her ground, fight her corner, as she always did when faced with confrontation.

"He is just playing with your love of drama, Joanne Hart," Reggie muttered. "Being a diva is fine, I can live with that. But this is such a dangerous and very expensive drama ... and because of the way things stand with Mr Bellosace, this story is not going to end well. There's not going to be any happily ever after ending to the Farrell story."

Joanne was silent but her eyes filled with tears as she surveyed her boots.

Angela looked mournfully at Reggie, who was still mopping up champagne as he spoke. He shrugged helplessly when he looked up and caught Angela's brown eyes.

"You will never get the Louis Vuitton contract while you are with this loser, Joey," he continued, hammering away at his key message.

Joanne glared at Reggie who noticed the tears welling in her eyes and her increasingly defensive body language. He softened his tone and, like the shrewd negotiator he was, switched to a more positive message.

"Louis Vuitton want you Joey. They want you to be the ambassador for their global branding campaign, but they told me again this morning they won't be risking their corporate reputation on a freak show."

He paused for a minute and let the ugly truth just hang there in the room.

"And I can't honestly say I blame them."

"Farrell is the deal breaker, he's the only thing standing in the way of you and Louis Vuitton working together," Reggie continued quietly.

Joanne gasped for air as a muscle painfully went into spasm. Two tears rolled almost unnoticed down her left cheek and she started to stroke her stomach with her left hand.

"You've always wanted to be the Louis Vuitton girl," Reggie continued coaxingly. "Louis Vuitton want you Joey. They are offering a $20 million four-year contract plus a Falcon 900 EX corporate jet with your face on the tail as private transport for all your official duties. We can close the deal with them next week. Please! Do yourself a favour. Think about it."

Angela looked at the dishevelled but defiant state of her friend and, having seen it all before, shook her head sadly. Yet the instant she looked away in dismay there was a slight involuntary nodding of Joanne's head and a glimmer of recognition in her eyes.

"Oooooooohh. She just will not listen, Reggie," Angela suggested softly. "It is like some kind of 'orrible Shakespearian tragedy."

Joanne straightened her body - drew deeply on the show-must-go-on ethos that had seen her survive and thrive in the fashion industry snake pit for seven long years - and fixed first Angela and then Reggie with her best 'don't go there' smile.

Joanne, now the method actor on autopilot, adopted a mock-earnest tone and craftily side-stepped the question of her nightmare love interest altogether.

"Media training for Hannah you say? Will Grant still work with us after this naughty French girl shagged him and ran?"

Joanne smiled, sweet and defiant, as she pushed her right index finger in and gently stroked Angela's nose.

The conversation was off the thin-ice and onto detail. Point made, Reggie surrendered the moment, sat down and sipped some champagne from his glass. Joanne scoffed a piece of sushi. Angela seemed mildly amused.

"The poor man is besotted. He wants more! "Reggie teased.

Reggie and Joanne roared with laughter. Angela stroked her hair and grinned through pursed lips. "A little decorum, s'il vous plaît," she replied evenly.

Joanne and Reggie chuckled but their tone was gentler. Angela bit into half a piece of sushi and pointed back at her partner in crime. Joanne ducked the finger, slid closer to Reggie and sipped on her champagne.

"So we do Hannah?" Reggie asked, aiming his rhetorical question squarely at Joanne.

"So we do Hannah!" she agreed instantly, a charming grin upon her face.

Reggie switched his stare of intent to Angela. Joanne threw a sisterly arm around her and Angela's radiant smile suddenly lit up the room.

"Like the pretty American woman said," Angela responded in a folksy manner, "we do 'Annah!"

Reggie smiled at his charges. "Right, well, now that's sorted, let's get the stars of the show back to their party, shall we?"

"Just let me fix my face," Joanne replied and reached for her bag. Her friends sat quietly watching. Joanne stared into a compact mirror and after a moment dabbing at her mascara-stained eyes with a cotton wool bud, she told Reggie firmly: "I do want the Louis Vuitton contract."

She looked up at him.

"I will sort things out Reggie, I promise."

Reggie, stone faced, immediately thrust forward his right hand. "We have a deal?" he asked seriously and stared earnestly into her eyes.

Joanne took his hand in hers and shook it firmly. "Deal," she replied and nodded.

Minutes later Angela, Joanne and Reggie returned to Model Citizens Inc's raucously partying function room.

Grabbing fresh flutes of champagne from the tray of a passing waiter, they dived enthusiastically into the adoring crowd.

The room burst into sustained applause and a few of the young Turks rhythmically stomped their feet on the floor. Joanne raised both her hands triumphantly in the air and then, with an ironic laugh, lowered her hands and checked her breasts were still securely nestled inside her cocktail dress.

The crowd roared with supportive laughter as the wall of cameras zoomed in on LA's IT girl.

Reggie guided Angela and Joanne through the back slapping crowd towards Hannako, an alluring

Eurasian photographic model the agency had signed up earlier that day.

Hannako was standing with the unflappable Francis, the Model Citizens Office Manager, by a side table that the caterers were busy restocking with champagne, vodka and mountains of delicious organic finger food.

19 years of age and a thin five foot two inches tall, Hannako was wearing a tiered transparent black Dior chiffon skirt and short-sleeved black Dior snakeskin jacket, a large red Japanese hair clasp set off her jet-black hair and a pair of light blue Christian Louboutin heels perfectly enclosed her dainty feet.

Francis, an elegant 36-year-old blonde former model, wore blue Capital E jeans, a black pima cotton Model Citizens polo shirt with blue sleeves and red branding, a silver Tondo watch, a subtle wedding ring and no-brand black tennis shoes.

Angela walked up to Francis, nodded and genuinely hugged her. "Bonsoir, Francis. 'Ow are you?"

"Bonsoir, Ang, congratulations," she replied face-to-face. "I'm so pleased for you!" As Angela and Francis kissed, French style, Reggie moved into the space between the gang of four. He tried not to notice that Joanne and Francis were obviously feuding and ignoring each other again.

"Sorry guys I have to get to an urgent meeting in New York," Reggie announced apologetically. "But I wanted to make sure that Angela and Joanne met Hannako. She signed with us just a few hours ago and I believe that one day soon, she'll make the same elite league as you two."

Hannako blushed. Francis nodded. Reggie smiled knowingly in turn at Angela, Joanne and finally Hannako.

"You know Ang, Hannako reminds me a whole lot of you when you first joined team Model Citizens two years ago," he said.

Angela and Joanne laughed.

"Uh oh," Joanne replied to Reggie as she eyed Hannako, and then Angela, suspiciously.

"She's got that same X factor. The camera loves her too, and I want my two Super Models to make her feel right at home, OK," Reggie continued.

Angela, Joanne, Francis and Hannako were all smiles for the man.

"Sorry, I've really got to go catch this flight. I'll call you guys later." Reggie waved to the group and whispered something in Francis' ear.

"Joanne, can you drop by the office around five tomorrow afternoon?" he asked.

"Sure Reg," she replied in characteristic cheeky fashion.

"Great, see you tomorrow. Have a wonderful night everyone and Joanne, Angela, please do enjoy this moment."

Reggie laid a happy smile upon the group, kissed Angela tenderly on both cheeks, turned smoothly on the balls of his feet and in an instant was gone. Angela, Joanne and Francis watched as Reggie floated politely through the crowd, meeting and greeting as he went.

Hannako stared, intrigued, at Angela.

Angela turned her head and curiously surveyed Hannako's face.

"'Annako, you finished second in the Estee Lauder Awards, yes?"

"Yes, yes I did, but I had no chance against you guys," she replied humbly.

Angela and Joanne smiled warmly at the awe-struck Hannako. Joanne kissed her lightly on the lips and, while in close, stroked her ass with her left hand.

"I think we are going to get along, Heather," Joanne said patronisingly in her best alpha Queen tone.

Joanne put a fraternal arm around Hannako's shoulder, the other around Angela's. The trio offered professional smiles to the cameras. As the space around Angela and Joanne rapidly filled with well wishers and new friends, Angela smiled at Hannako and Joanne patted Angela on the bottom while she stared appreciatively at the new girl's physique.

"My name is Hannako," was her confused reply. Joanne shrugged. "OK, so text me Hannako, Francis has my number," she replied.

With that, Joanne took Angela by the hand and led her off to the next networking opportunity in the crowded space. Hannako glanced at the disappearing Super Models, then looked uncertainly at Francis, who shrugged nonchalantly, rolled her eyes and smiled.

"You have such a beautiful name, what does it mean?" Francis asked.

Hannako's pronounced cheeks flushed beet red and she glanced downward. "Please don't laugh. My parents were, like, total hippies when they were younger," she replied. Francis nodded empathetically.

"It means flower child in Japanese," she explained.

"That's gorgeous, Hannako," Francis replied. "It's memorable and really groovy!" She smiled reassuringly and they both laughed at her joke.

"Hey, while we have got the chance, can I introduce you to some photographers?" "That would be totally awesome," Hannako replied excitedly and nodded. "Austin," Francis called out to a giant of a man dressed in a dark Black Label Calvin Klein suit, lurid psychedelic top hat and purple formal

Louis Vuitton shoes. Austin, who at that moment was taking a tall glass of vodka from a caterer just a metre away, spun around.

"Yes Francis," he said.

"Have you got a moment? There's a special someone here I want you to meet."

"Splendid" replied the cat in the hat and walked their way. "Who have we here Francis?" he asked.

"Hannako, meet Austin, advertising photographer extraordinaire," Francis said and smiled like a proud matriarch as the pair air kissed.

Austin looked the latest Model Citizen up and down approvingly. "You are absolutely fabulous, darling," he advised Hannako. "Your look is just what I need. Are you available for a Macy's catalogue shoot next Wednesday?"

"Yes I am," Hannako said quietly and smiled.

"Great. Excellent. Consider yourself booked, darling. We are on location from 9am," Austin informed Hannako and put his long bohemian arm around her shoulder.

"I will sort the details with Francis in the morning."

"You got yourself a deal Austin," Francis replied.

"Thank you so much for this opportunity Austin," Hannako schmoozed as she stared up at her first Model Citizens client.

"I've always been fascinated by advertising. It's such an exciting business! Please tell me everything about what you do," she asked the lanky photographer.

Francis smiled admiringly as her new mannequin turned on the charm. "You will go far, flower child," she thought to herself and, leaving the pair to get acquainted, moved to work the other side of the room.

MR FOOTBALL HAD DEAD EYES

Two days later, Angela drove her canary-yellow V6 Renault Laguna Coupe up onto the half-full top deck of the LA Eagles Football Club parking lot. It was around an hour before afternoon training was due to begin and small groups of players were arriving at the club.

Angela wore a home-made boho denim micro mini skirt, a baggy black Givenchy t-shirt and black Kung Fu shoes. Her lips were red and full Lancôme makeup highlighted her perfect high cheekbones and facial features.

She parked her new sports car next to Brett Farrell's huge red Ford F650 SUV in an isolated corner of the grey concrete parking bay that had a view out over the playing arena.

The moment Angela stepped out of her car she was confronted from behind by Brett. "Hello, welcome, so great to see you again," he said in an abrasive, nasal tone. Angela spun around on the balls of her feet, perfectly balanced, and instinctively brought her open hands up defensively in front of her chest.

Wearing the Eagles blue and yellow number 1 jumper, long sky blue pants and red and white boots, Brett towered over Angela. He carried a Canon EOS 5D Mark II digital camera that he waved under her nose.

"Funny you should ring and want to talk to me today Angelina. Your timing is real good, cos I got something I want to talk to you about too."

Angela scowled, took a step back and shook her head at him. "I don't like you calling me Angelina, that's my mama's name, you know that," she replied.

"Whatever." Brett shrugged and smirked. He turned the camera on, pressed a couple of buttons and handed it to Angela. "Hehe, check out Joey's Hollywood debut."

Angela stared at the screen. Brett laughed cruelly as the film of him whipping Joanne played before Angela's disbelieving eyes.

"Joanne's right into pain, I bet you didn't know that did you?"

Brett paused and allowed the appalled Angela to watch several minutes of his amateur pornography.

While she watched, shrouded in an indignant silence, Brett noticed three of his uniformed teammates emerging from a large white Ford van 100 metres away. He observed the players backslapping and joking as they unloaded a number of bags full of football gear.

Angela made a loud hissing noise that drew Brett's attention back to her.

"Do you think she'll win an Oscar for that performance Angelina? Does the porn industry do awards like the Oscars? I figured a slut like you would know."

Angela glared at him. "Oh hang on, silly me," Brett said with a smirk. He chuckled and slapped his thighs with both hands.

"You would have to grow some tits before you could become a porn star wouldn't you, poor little Angelina."

She stood her ground in a karate-fighting stance - powerfully balanced, left knee bent forward, right leg straight back - holding the camera, refusing to be intimidated.

"You are sick, yes, you are pure evil," Angela growled coldly and quietly, staring defiantly into his dead eyes.

Brett laughed out loud.

"Why thank you, skank. You know coming from you, I'll take that as a fucking compliment," Brett replied and rubbed his hands together as he took a large step closer towards her. "So here's my question for you Angelina. You wanna play porn stars with Brett? How about it skank?"

"You are out of your fucking mind, cochon. You need psychiatrique help," Angela snarled and turned toward her car. Brett grabbed her upper right arm and painfully dug his powerful fingers deep into her bicep muscle.

With sheer brute force, he dragged her unwilling feet across the concrete floor; forced her body to move closer to his.

"Maybe we could open the film with a bondage threesome scene? You two hung from a butcher's rack? Me wearing a devil's mask and apron? I know Joey would like that. Hell yeah. You know she's always talking about you."

With his free hand, Brett slapped her hard on the bottom.

"Let go of me you animal," Angela yelled and tried unsuccessfully to prise his hand off her arm. "Give me the camera, bitch and then, maybe, I will let you go," he replied.

As Angela struggled to escape from his powerful vice like grip, a crooked grin spread across his face.

"No Angelina, no. That's not going to help resolve our situation. You gotta be nice and polite to Brett. You gotta give Brett his camera," he said patronisingly.

Angela spat in his face. "Only in your sick dreams," she hollered as loud as she could. "Oh, I love you even more when you get angry, sweet tiny tits Angelina," he replied mockingly and smacked her ass three more times.

Angela screamed as piercingly and long as her lungs were capable of. Brett just laughed heartlessly. While still holding her firmly by the arm, he turned his hips to face her and confidently reached for the camera, a narcissistic grin welded to his bruised face.

Maintaining full eye contact, Angela threw a snap kick at her tormentor. Her right leg crashed into his groin. Her right foot made full contact and, with a well timed thrust of her hips, Angela rode the kick all the way home like she had never done before in training.

Brett yelped, released his grip on her arm and fell in a dysfunctional heap on the oil-stained parking lot floor. It was only after he hit the concrete that Angela registered the sound of people running towards her from behind.

Within seconds three uniformed and helmeted LA Eagles footballers - Buddy, GW and Paulie - were standing beside Angela, surveying the over-glorified oxygen thief laying before them.

"Is everything OK, ma'am," Buddy, a mountain of a man, asked her.

Brett writhed on the floor, gasping for breath, clutching at his bruised balls. He moaned but was speechless. Angela moved next to Buddy and stared up at him.

"No. No, it's not OK. Please help me. This animal attacked me. Please stay 'ere and make sure I can get in my car and leave. Please, help me, all I want to do is leave, get away from this monster."

"Help me, help me," Brett whispered to his colleagues as loud as he could from the foetal position he was curled into at their feet but no one heard him.

The footballers only had eyes for Angela.

“I’m real sorry, ma’am, on behalf of the Eagles, on behalf of all of us. This loser don’t speak for us, please believe me. There’s something wrong with his mind,” Buddy said slowly.

“I want you to know Brett wasn’t always this way ma’am. His head took a real big hit in the 2007 Super Bowl and, ever since that day, he has been real fucked up,” Paulie added insightfully.

“Oh really?” Angela replied. She glanced contemptuously at the disgraced footballer.

“That’s no excuse for his behaviour toward you ma’am,” Buddy said and shook his head. He motioned for his teammates to step forward and the three footballers formed a line of steeled muscle between Angela and Brett.

Buddy stood over his fallen teammate. “You are free to leave, ma’am. This pig won’t harm you no more, you have my personal guarantee of that. We’re going to teach him a good lesson, right now,” Buddy said and kicked the prone Mr Football in the ass.

“Thank you,” Angela replied and stepped forward. She looked into Buddy’s eyes, touched him gratefully on the arm.

“Much obliged ma’am,” he said, handed Angela his card and pitched her a deep and meaningful smile. “You ring me if you ever have any more trouble with this loser, OK?”

Angela agreed she would and ran straight for her car. Buddy leaned forward and got right into Brett’s face.

“You suck Farrell,” he yelled at his teammate who was playing dead, trying yet again to manipulate his way out of trouble. Buddy grabbed him by the scruff of the jumper and started shaking his former hero as if he was a piece of white trash.

Angela jumped into her car, put the camera and Buddy's card in the glove box, pushed the key into the ignition, revved the engine frantically and began to reverse away. As she did so, Buddy and GW were taking turns at punching Brett in the stomach. Paulie was just standing there, sadly, head bowed, struggling with mixed emotions.

Angela glanced with satisfaction at the karmic payback through her rear vision mirror. And, with a screech of the tyres, brought her Renault to a stop.

"Not so tough now are you?" she yelled out the window, recycling the line she had heard Brett using to humiliate her lover.

Angela put her foot down hard and the yellow coupe's tyres spun and smoked as she raced away from the LA Eagles Football Club toward sanity and safety.

WE ARE CELEBRITIES NOW

The next day Joanne and Angela were backstage at ABC's LA TV studios, sitting in wide comfortable chairs in front of a wall of mirrors, getting prepared for their Hannah interview. Two make-up artists, dressed in black Levi jeans and white ABC branded polo shirts, were applying lotions and deploying hair dryers.

Another two women wearing white cotton kimonos were massaging Angela's feet. A third woman, the segment stylist, dressed in a white ABC polo, red Levi jeans and carrying a large red security swipe around her neck, arrived on the scene. She presented the Super Models with a cheery smile and a sliver tray on which sat a steaming silver pot of freshly brewed green tea and two small white cups.

Joanne was dressed in smart casual style: blue Levi skinny jeans, white Yves St Laurent long-sleeved cotton shirt and white Onitsuka Tiger shoes.

Angela was seriously hung-over. After succeeding in her confrontation with Brett, there had been so much adrenalin surging around her body it had taken three bottles of Bordeaux red wine to push her into sleep.

Six hours later, Angela was feeling more than a little nauseous and wished she was still home in bed. She refused to pull up her pants when the stylist asked her. Angela just sat there uncomfortably pointing at her stomach in a Rigby & Peller purple and black lace bustier, black lace Aubade knickers, matching stockings and yellow Prada trousers that were down around her ankles.

"I've got it bad, mademoiselle. Mon stomach it aches, yes," Angela moaned. The stylist and foot masseurs exchanged knowing glances as her gastric zone rumbled noisily.

"Ooooooohh," Angela cried out.

"Watch out," the stylist said to the masseurs who, just in time, managed to move before Angela vomited noisily. She sprayed a curdled red black liquid all over the vanity station, her legs and trousers and the carpet in front of her.

Joanne, appalled, jumped out of her chair with an offended cry as foul smelling fluid dribbled from Angela's nose. Her overloaded, dehydrated body flopped back limply into the chair.

"I can't take you anywhere girl," Joanne chided her friend angrily. "What the fuck is Hannah going to think of us?"

"I'm so sorry," Angela mumbled in reply. The two dressers looked at each other and rolled their eyes.

Joanne held her nose with two fingers of her right hand. "That's really going to help isn't it?" she snapped.

"Excusez-moi mademoiselles, please forgive me," Angela quietly begged the support staff. "I will pay any dry cleaning costs you 'ave, yes."

"It's OK Angela," replied the stylist, placing one of the masseur's hands on her shoulders. "It's OK. Just relax. Take some nice deep breaths and we will give you a massage. You will feel so-oh much better ..."

Just 90 minutes later and it was show time!

The Hannah juggernaut was ready to go to live to camera in front of a large studio audience. On the familiar lavish set, Angela and Joanne were sitting happily on either side of the Queen of daytime TV's empty throne.

Both Super Models were dressed to impress. Angela's priceless blue silk taffeta Dior dinner dress that Reggie has bought her was full in length and set off her silver and red Garrard's Heart of the Kingdom Ruby necklace and shiny black vinyl Louboutin stiletto platform boots.

Joanne pitched in a "trust me" white Versace shift dress, cut high and low, a white gold diamond cross pendant on slender gold chain around her neck, red Christian Dior heels on her slender feet and lips that shone diplomatically red with Estee Lauder gloss.

During the 10-minute pre-show audience rev up, Angela and Joanne had been flirting shamelessly with Hannah's drooling warm up guy - a ponytailed 30-something charmer who wore red Levi jeans, an extra large white ABC polo and a red security swipe hanging from his hairy neck.

But now it really was show time. The theme music came up. The On Air light above the Studio One doors turned red as inside the house lights went down and a single dazzling spotlight shone on the warm up artist.

"Thanks everyone! Now without further ado, it's show time! Would you all please make some noise for HAN-NAH!" the warm up guy enthused.

Suddenly, bathed in the spotlight, Queen Hannah strode regally onstage to a rapturous and contagious form of audience adulation. Her studio band played a short and powerful piece of music.

As usual, Hannah looked the part: as understated as you can be wearing pearls and a lilac Prada ensemble, flat Ferragamo suede shoes and a long cascading Afro hairstyle. The high priest of African-American soft power packed a hell of a lot into five feet six inches of athletic body.

She perched on the stage and smoothly soaked up the adoring energy of another "full house" audience.

"Thanks you ... Thank you ... Hello everyone and welcome to the first Hannah show for another week."

She waved in acknowledgement to her loyal band, turned and smiled at the audience before settling down upon her throne.

"As regular viewers know, we like to keep up with all the latest news from the wonderful world of fashion."

Hannah beamed and paused as she pointed Angela and then Joanne out to camera 3.

Angela was sporting a nervous half-smile - her stomach was still rumbling away - while Joanne's "pick me Louis Vuitton" pout was turned up to high-beam.

"And joining me today, for an exclusive interview, are the two hottest faces in modelling right now: LA's Joanne Hart and, from France, Angela Durand."

Audience applause folded seamlessly into background footage that showed one minute of highlights of both girl's modelling careers and ended with pictures of Joanne and Brett standing together at a New York nightclub. Angela momentarily lost her smile when she saw the footballer's smirking face.

"Please join with me in making Joanne and Angela feel welcome everyone," the host with the most said. As the crowd clapped and whistled, Hannah rose and air kissed the pair. The band played funk.

"In case you missed it, my two guests made history this week by becoming the first ever joint-winners of the Estee Lauder International Modelling Awards," Hannah announced admiringly.

"Congratulations Angela, Joanne, and welcome to you both. It's great to finally make you a part of the show."

The audience response was enthusiastic. The stars from Model Citizens turned on their most professional smiles and most engaging body language.

"Why thank you, Hannah," Joanne replied coyly and Angela, in awe of the biggest name in daytime television, nodded respectfully to host and audience before delicately placing both hands on her right thigh.

"Joanne how did it feel to win one of the coveted Estee Lauder awards? To be the historic first ever joint-winner with your friend Angela?" Hannah asked.

Joanne leant back in her chair momentarily, then tilted forward from the hips and bowed her head in contemplation, pausing before she answered.

"It feels kinda unreal Hannah. It's like a dream come true but I'm still, like, pinching myself. The phone has not stopped ringing. So many people want to say 'you go girl'."

"How's suddenly becoming a Super Model working out for you Angela?" Hannah asked.

"I'm not sure if it has sunk in yet for either of us," she replied. "But many old friends have been calling, yes, and I have been offered some wonderful new jobs."

Joanne leant forward. She raised her right hand. She jumped in.

"Me too. What was I saying?" her index finger resting on her bottom lip, country-style. "We have both worked so hard to master the fashion business Hannah and the awards are recognition of how far we have come as models and as women."

"That's wonderful," Hannah replied. "Before we go on, in case some of our viewers missed the 2009 Estee Lauder International Modelling Awards broadcast here in America on the ABC network, let's take a look at some pictures from the big night."

Angela and Joanne relived their night of nights watching televised highlights with Hannah and 100 million of her close personal friends scattered all round the world. The interviews, the strutting contestants, the acceptance speeches, Joanne's wardrobe malfunction, were all flashed across the small screen.

When two minutes of highlights finished, as the audience applauded the glamorous illusion and Joanne sulked about the tit shot, Hannah looked maternally at Angela. Her research manager had definitely earned her money that day.

"What a wonderful moment for you both. Angela, how do your parents feel about your win?"

"Oooooooohh, 'Annah, my mama could not stop crying and telling me how proud she was. When I was just a girl, she worked two jobs to pay for me to go to modelling and yoga school. None of this could have happened without 'er. That's why I can't forget about 'er now, 'Annah! Now I am suddenly a rich woman, with the money I won from the Estee Lauder Awards I have decided to buy 'er and papa a new house on the Riviera."

"Does your mom know about this?" Hanna asked.

"Non. Err, no, not yet," Angela replied and smiled: dreamily and misty-eyed. Hannah smiled back respectfully. Entranced. Joanne suffered a moment of spotlight deprivation syndrome and stiffened as Hannah eyed-balled her studio audience and pushed the human-interest angle.

"That is so-oh incredibly heart-warming. You heard it first here everyone."

The audience cooed appreciatively and Hannah moved to the edge of her throne to get just a little closer to her warm, charming guest.

"What a loving daughter you are," she told camera 1.

Angela was touched. Hannah swept her right hand from the direction of the audience towards and past the sulky Joanne and back to highlight the young woman who had suddenly become France's most popular ambassador to the United States of America.

"What is your mom's name?"

"Her name is Angelina, 'Annah."

"Angelina? What would Angelina say to you if she could be here with you right now?"

Angela put her right index finger to her bottom lip as she considered her answer to the question. Joanne was fidgeting.

"Oooooooohh, Angelique, I just want you to be happy in this life," Angela replied dreamily.

"And what would you like to say to your mom right now?" Hannah continued.

"Mama, I love you so very much, je t'adore, thank you. Thank you for everything you have done for me. Without you, I would be nothing," she said with a lump in her throat and a tear of joy glistening in her left eye.

"I have so much to tell you, oui. Please send my love to papa and Odette ..." she concluded and camera 2 captured the most sincere and moving smile anyone would witness that day.

Hannah turned and smiled at camera 3 as Angela shared her billion dollar smile with the world. In contrast, Joanne appeared a little bored. "I am not surprised that Angelina is so proud of you, Angela, she has raised an extraordinary young woman," Hannah concluded.

Angela's still pale face blushed as the audience applauded and Hannah highlighted both Model Citizens with her arms.

"Angela, Joanne, as there is so much interest in your stories I do hope both of you will be able to stay with us for a little longer today and, maybe later, answer some questions from your many new fans in our audience?" Hannah enquired.

Both Model Citizens nodded enthusiastically and Hannah leant back in her throne and smiled straight into camera 4.

"We are going to take a short message from our sponsors, but we'll be right back so don't go away y'all," she purred and the band started to play as the broadcast cut to a television advertisement for a "new and improved" Estee Lauder mascara product.

At that moment, Giselle Richter was sitting at her ostentatious corporate desk, staring at her computer screen and a sexy website picture of Joanne. A desktop TV monitor showed her the Hannah Show broadcast.

Dressed in a grey AGB two button suit jacket and matching box pleat skirt, white shirt and her Stuart Weitzman Retro Rose pumps, Giselle was not in a sharing and caring mood.

"Screw you, Joanne Hart. You are going down," she snorted, pointing her left index finger at Joanne's striking face on the TV. "One way or another, I swear, revenge will be mine."

Just a little further into the Hannah Show and the audience questions segment was almost complete. Angela was wooing the crowd.

"Yes, 'Annah, I always encourage girls who want to get involved with the wonderful world of modelling to start with grooming and deportment courses and, err, to practice living with cameras so you can learn to become comfortable around them."

"Dreams can come true, yes?" Angela purred in her soft and beguiling, chocolate-coated throaty tone. "In life, you just 'ave to believe. You 'ave to dare to dream."

As the audience roared its approval, Hannah leant forward to camera 3, asserting her control over the moment. Angela smiled at the audience and Joanne crossed and uncrossed her legs competitively.

"How will success change you both? Will you be the same women 12 months from now?" the host asked.

Angela and Joanne nodded in agreement with each other. Their extensive media training kicked in. Angela motioned to her partner.

"Après vous, Joey," she said.

"Don't you love French," Hannah informed her audience. "It's such a poetic language."

As Hannah engaged her viewers, Joanne jumped in.

"Oh yes, French sounds so sexy Hannah. In answer to your question, we're just ordinary women who have worked hard to create opportunities for ourselves."

The studio burst into spontaneous applause. Onstage, there were self-satisfied grins aplenty.

"Nothing much is gonna change. We're gonna keep working real hard for a living, Hannah, you can be sure of that," Joanne said smoothly. "Oui ..." Angela agreed and nodded.

"She means yes," Hannah said cheerily.

"Thank you Joanne and Angela for sharing your success with us today, it's been wonderful to have you both on the show."

The ABC band struck up a bright tune while Hannah fiddled with her earpiece. Her producer suggested they go with the flow.

"My producer says we have time for one more question." Hannah said and the audience murmured in agreement with their Queen.

"Madame, yes, the woman with the orange bag. Hello, you have a question for our guests?" Hannah asked.

The questioner was an eccentrically dressed, 60-something member of the overly sincere hippie generation, a personal Hannah plant, who had been sitting in the middle of the audience waiting for her cue.

She rose to speak, dressed in a rainbow coloured kaftan, blue Faberge jeans and sporting big blonde hair. She carefully took the microphone an attendant passed to her.

"Thank you Hannah, I love your show. My question is for Joanne. Why are you dating such a violent, misogynist footballer? Don't you understand, now you are a Super Model, you now have serious social responsibilities because you are such a powerful role model for millions of impressionable young American girls?"

The microphone was abruptly turned off and the spotlight returned to the stage. Hannah immediately worked the crowd and the Model Citizens who appeared, temporarily, frozen in the spotlight.

"I gotta say I think that's a real tough question," Hannah empathised.

Joanne nodded vigorously. Angela leant pensively back in her chair. Even though they had practiced these sorts of questions during three media skills workshops with Grant, Angela was worried about how her volatile friend would respond as her wine-induced throbbing headache headed for migraine territory.

Joanne frowned and gently stroked her stomach in a circular motion with her right hand. Hanna personalised the storyline.

"You know, I once stepped out with a major league basketball player," Hannah said in her best confessional style. "We had photographers following us everywhere. The newspapers started quoting 'friends' I did not realise I had, talking about arguments which never happened, about babies and other women and all kinds of other things that were entirely imaginary." She rolled her eyes and hunched up her shoulders in exasperation. Everyone chuckled at Hannah's joke as she paused with devastating effect. Well, almost everyone. Joanne looked like she would rather be somewhere else.

"This was happening almost every day for four months. We both found it a very tough position to be in. The media literally threw our relationship on the fire and burnt it."

Hannah momentarily seemed transported back to that tempestuous time and her face softened.

Angela smiled reassuringly at Joanne as Hannah snapped back to the task at hand. Her demeanour rapidly morphed from confidant to prosecutor.

"But being a celebrity has many down-sides," she said deliberately. "There's a price to be paid for fame. You know, you do get all sorts of unwanted attention. I have come to realise that losing your privacy, sadly, goes with having a prominent position in our society."

Joanne's head had tilted forward and she was ever so slightly shaking it in disbelief.

Angela smiled in a forced professional way, trying to cover for her brooding friend. Hannah, paused, let the tension build and went after the big storyline.

"So, Joanne, given all the ugly media headlines that Brett Farrell attracted again this week, we are all interested to know how you cope with a boyfriend who appears to have quite serious anger-management issues?"

Joanne thought of the Holy Grail, the Louis Vuitton contract, and in that moment turned her discomfort into the opportunity of a lifetime. She remembered the media drills and straightened her posture but kept her head just slightly bowed to ensure she came across like the humble girl next door she was not.

"He's my ex boyfriend, Hannah. It's, like, really disappointing. I win a huge Award, make history and all the media seems to want to do is dig up dirt on my ex."

Hannah lobbed her response straight back over the net. "That must hurt?" she asked her precocious guest.

"It does hurt Hannah. It is so-oh unfair. I've worked so hard to get where I am and now some people in the media just want to, like, shred me."

A solitary tear ran down Joanne's left cheek in close-up. Angela and Hannah nodded in agreement. The audience cooed sympathetically.

"I left Brett Farrell two months ago, long before any of the mafia stuff came along. It's like that song said: I used to love him but it's all over now."

Having delivered her rehearsed lines, she nodded uncertainly toward her host and friend. And fell silent.

"So what advice would you offer to a young woman with an abusive boyfriend?" Hannah asked camera 1.

"Just leave him!" Joanne replied, her body language more hesitant than her words.

"How did you walk out on Mr Football?"

Joanne fluttered her eyes and took a deep breath before she replied. "First, Hannah, I had to learn to like myself more. With the help of my friends."

Joanne's voice was cracking so she paused, glanced at Angela and then looked down into her lap.

She sat still and sombre for a moment. While she collected her thoughts, Joanne paraded her vulnerability for camera 4 like her genuinely red-raw soul was just another frock.

"Then as my self esteem improved, I just woke up to how abusive our relationship had become. One night about eight weeks ago he, he, he hit me and threatened to damage my face so badly I would not be able to model anymore. So the next day I packed my bags and moved out of the Malibu apartment we had shared."

Joanne dabbed at her nose with a white cotton handkerchief. Hannah looked on sympathetically as she hung back and let the author unfold her story.

"I'm still struggling with the grief and the confusion, Hannah. How could I have let myself fall so low? I still don't really know the answer to that question."

Joanne started sobbing and sniffing; tears ran down both her cheeks. She had seriously let her guard down on network television and suddenly, at this moment of deep Oprah-style confession, she worried about how Brett was going to react?

"I still have feelings of inadequacy ... I ... I ..." Joanne stammered and then broke into a little theatrical sob. Caught up in her own story, a very real fear of Brett clouded her thoughts.

"My counsellor has been working very closely with me on getting through this terrible ordeal, one day at a time. But it has been terrible, Hannah. My poor little heart can't stand much more of it ..."

Joanne buried her head in her hands and sobbed loudly and genuinely.

In front of a global television audience of 100 million people, she had never felt so lost and so alone. Her body was visibly shaking. Hannah led the audience in supportive applause.

"I very much admire your courage and determination, Joanne, and thank you so much for your honesty," Hannah said, a look of maternal concern transplanted onto her face as she continued to clap.

Angela stood up from her chair, walked across the stage to Joanne, knelt down in front of her and threw her arms tenderly around her friend and comforted her as best she could.

Sensing a ratings bonanza, Hannah said nothing. She sat passively and watched. After their lingering embrace, Angela turned towards Hannah.

"Please stop, 'Annah, no more questions, please. It is so cruel, can you not see her pain?" she pleaded politely.

The room gasped, some in the audience whispered, as the Model Citizens soap opera headed into unscripted territory.

Joanne stared deeply into Angela's big brown eyes. For the first time in her chaotic life, she could feel the wonderful warmth of unconditional love. As Hannah's cameras feasted greedily on the endearing melodrama, Joanne relaxed and surrendered to the overwhelming sense of sweet salvation that surged right through her.

Hannah sighed and raised both hands. Her palms pointed forward towards the Model Citizens in a gesture of surrender.

Joanne smiled serenely through her tears at her inquisitor.

"Hannah, I am so-oh lucky to have Angela as my best friend," she spluttered.

Angela smiled right back and stroked her hand reassuringly. Joanne gazed at Angela, kissed her full on the lips and stroked her left cheek tenderly. "Thank you, French girl" she said quietly, captured by camera 3's full close up shot.

Uptown, a red-faced Giselle Richter screeched with disgust at her office TV screen, punched the remote control with a fat finger and turned off the Hannah Show.

Back in ABC's LA Studio One, Hannah concluded in concise style: "You are very lucky, Joanne, for even in your hour of darkness, you are not alone. Please thank Angela and Joanne for being with us today everyone."

The audience gave Angela and Joanne the kind of standing ovation that their two Oscar-winning performances deserved. Hannah moved next to Joanne and embraced her. Angela, stood up from her crouching position and beamed. "Thank you for being so open about your situation Joanne," Hanna said, staring purposefully into camera 2.

"May God bless you. You have helped so many other women today by being so honest."

"I think it's so very important for all of us to remember that, sadly, the problem of domestic violence is everywhere in our society. It's important for all of us to remember to reach out for help, if we find ourselves in a troubled relationship," Hannah noted.

"Please take good care of yourself Joanne. And do remember you are surrounded by lots of good people, like Angela, who obviously care very much about you ..."

Hannah moved to Angela, who had, unprompted, returned to her seat. She grasped both her hands and squeezed them gently.

"Thank you, Angela." Hannah said and kissed her shy guest affectionately on both cheeks. Then the television host smiled at camera 1 and turned to face her enchanted audience.

"Joanne, Angela, we will look forward to following your careers. We'll be watching out for you, both of you, and cheering you on as you consolidate your position in that small and elite group of global Super Models."

The audience continued to loudly support the girls from Model Citizens. Some women in the front rows of the studio appeared, like Angela and Joanne, to be genuinely overcome with emotion.

Reggie the cynic had been shaken and stirred. Sitting there like a worried parent in a black Armani suit, red trilby hat, red Prada shirt and posh black Footprints shoes, Reggie dabbed at his wet eyes with a red cotton handkerchief.

"Thank you Joanne, thank you Angela, for having taken time out of your busy schedules to visit with us today and for sharing with us such extraordinary insights into your incredible journeys to the top," Hannah continued.

"I can assure you that the Hannah website has already come alive. My viewers have been deeply moved by your stories of hope and courage. You guys will be pleased to know that the majority of posters on my blog see both of you as role models for the next generation of young women."

Angela and Joanne put on a good show of humility as they absorbed the avalanche of approval.

Joanne's face glistened with tears. Her mascara had run and the hard exterior she had worn as a shield all her adult life melted. At that moment Joanne was certain, in her mind, that life would never be the same again.

Hannah pressed her hands together in front of her chest as she moved to "wrap up" the day's episode.

"Can I conclude by saying I am really looking forward to having you both on the program again soon."

Everyone applauded. Hannah put her arms out and touched Angela and Joanne's shoulders. Reggie looked like he had just won the lottery.

"Bye bye everyone, thank you so much for being a part of The Hannah Show today."

All three women arose from chairs and thrones to wave and acknowledge the caring audience.

Then Hannah, in close up, nodded to camera 4.

"Tomorrow, I will be talking to President Obama and Bono about hunger in the Horn of Africa, please join me then."

The tireless audience continued to applaud as the band played and The Hannah Show credits ran, bringing to a dramatic conclusion Hannah's highest rating episode for 2009.

Forty five minutes later and Giselle Richter had showered and changed in her corporate suite and was back slouched at her desk, wearing a green and white printed von Furstenberg dress and the Stuart Weitzman pumps, holding her 'secure' landline telephone to her left ear.

On her computer screen was a picture of Joanne, posing with Mickey and Minnie Mouse outside Disneyland, dressed in blue Wrangler jeans, red white and blue checked shirt and a straw country hat.

"Who is this?" Giselle demanded to know. The voice on the end of the line sounded vaguely familiar but the caller refused to identify himself.

Nonetheless she listened attentively before responding: "Hmmm, that's a really interesting story you got there, Mister whoever you are. I'd like to believe what you are telling me but what evidence have you got?"

She listened some more. "You what?" Giselle exclaimed in a loud and triumphant voice. "You got video of Hart and Verucce making out? Send it to me and I'll set the FBI right on them! Yeah. Absolutely. You have my personal guarantee of that."

"Yes, yep, email me the films via the corporate website. Yes, that's secure. Yeah that's best. Yes, yeah, right now would be perfect. Thank you."

Her secretary entered the room. Giselle scowled and waved him away.

A sadistic grin settled upon The Gale's face. She hadn't been so happy since the last time she had character assassinated a celebrity. She couldn't believe her luck.

“Good things come to managers who are prepared to shake the tree,” she thought.

Just a few minutes later and Giselle smiled like the cat that got the cream as she watched a film of Joanne - dressed in a white nurse’s uniform, a small white cap adorned with a red cross, and red fishnet stockings - providing Adam Verucce with oral sex as he lay on a child’s bed in a room full of dolls, teddy bears and sketches of ballerinas.

They were clearly getting down to it in the classy man’s family home.

Giselle watched with purely malicious intent as Joanne expertly brought Adam to orgasm, his puffed lips opening and closing.

Wearing just a white Ralph Lauren business shirt, the chubby little man gasped and groaned as he shot onto the now famous model’s face. Joanne grinned at her success.

“Oh Joey, I had forgotten just how good you make me feel,” Adam murmured and stroked her hair. “Why don’t we run away together? I’m so bored with Cindy and my whole goddam life.”

But Joanne was finished. There wasn’t going to be any rosy future, not for Adam. She licked her lips, kissed the hated designer lightly on his right cheek and smiled a hard-eyed ‘gotcha’ smile at the invisible camera.

Adam would soon discover this had been one seriously expensive blow-job.

When Brett had anonymously sent Joanne’s sordid Estee Lauder blackmail videos through to Giselle, he had no idea that his vengeful actions were going to backfire and the dogs would be set onto him as well. Then again, given the kamikaze state of mind Brett was in - after Joanne had dumped him live on America’s highest rating TV program - it probably would not have made much difference to the way he played his cards anyway.

After watching two short films of Adam and Joanne's antics, The Gale jumped back onto her secure corporate telephone line.

"Hi Tony, it's Giselle Richter ... Fine ... Fine, yes, and you?"

She listened briefly. "Sorry Tony, I'm in a hurry as usual. I need an information profile ... Yep, a full spectrum sweep, anything and everything. Her name is Joanne Hart, she's a model and I want whatever comes up on her boyfriend, Brett Farrell, too."

"Yeah, Mr Football, right. Whatever it takes, whatever it costs, just get me a dossier together as soon as you can. Yeah ... Understood ... Cost is not an issue here. Yeah, just bill the corporate account. I personally guarantee sign-off on all your expenses within 24 hours. I will email you through a purchase order within the hour," she promised and then listened for a minute.

"Yeah, there's a whole mess of dirt in this one Tony," Giselle drawled. "Hart has compromised my Awards and then there's that huge scandal with her goddam thug of a footballer boyfriend. To tell you the truth Tony, I want to crucify the bitch ... That's right ... Yeah."

Giselle paused and nodded into the phone "And just for the record, not a word to anyone Tony. This goddam situation is obviously real sensitive. Keep me posted buddy. Yep. As soon as you can ... Yeah ... Thanks. Bye."

The Gale placed the secure phone back into its cradle like it was a fragile hi-tech weapon she would soon be using again. She turned to her computer screen, called up Google and typed in the words Joanne Hart. She soon discovered there were

1,173,391 relevant pages and less than half of them related to the wardrobe malfunction.

Giselle sighed. She clicked on the first link and up came a picture of Joanne at a perfect beach, thigh deep in the crystal clear water, suggestively licking a lollipop in a cheeky red Cali Dreaming micro bikini.

Even though she had personally signed off on the cost of this photographic shoot which was part of an advertising campaign promoting Estee Lauder's new integrated skin care and sun protection product range, The Gale still shook her head in outrage and angrily declared: "You are riding for a fall, Hart."

Two hours later, Reggie was in his corporate limousine being driven to an uptown meeting with Chanel. He held in his hands an open copy of that invaluable masterpiece, Sun Tzu's book of strategy, *The Art Of War,* and was half-watching a TV screen in front of him as a *Fox Sports* reporter previewed the Super Bowl.

The breathless talking head was of the opinion that, if Brett Farrell played, the LA Eagles would win, a view not uncommon amongst the commentariat at the time.

"Despite his recent troubles, the club is confident Mr Football will play and lead his team to victory in the Super Bowl for the fourth time in the past five years."

Reggie clocked the action pictures of Brett on the screen and shook his head as the reporter's voice said: "The LA Eagles are set to become the most successful NFL team in American history thanks to Mr Football, Brett Farrell."

"I would not bet your house on that pal," Reggie spat at the *Fox Sport's* pictures of Brett, with a heavily bandaged head, standing next to media mogul Rupert Murdoch, in front of jubilant team-mates, club officials and an ecstatic stadium crowd. Mr Football had a deranged grin spread across his blood-smeared face as he waved the silver 2007 Vince Lombardi Super Bowl trophy above his head.

Reggie scowled and tapped his remote control. The channel changed and up popped Montgomery Burns and Homer Simpson.

Heading in the opposite direction, Angela and Joanne were sitting in the back of Martin's stretch limousine planning on partying "somewhere up-town."

Angela was dressed in a Lilac Givenchy couture dress, her prized peace sign sat on a short silver chain around her neck and she wore Lilac ballet shoes. Joanne bigged it up in low-slung red Marchesa dress, loud red Shiseido lips, silver and pearl Chopard earrings, black Rive Gauche silk and lace stockings and red Mai Lamore heels.

Pumped with the "live television" adrenalin rush, the Model Citizens had cranked up the volume of Curtis Mayfield's *Move On Up*.

"Bite your lip and take a trip
Though there may be wet road ahead
You cannot slip
Just move on up"

Both Angela and Joanne were holding long tall champagne glasses and flanked by two male Thai masseurs, wearing blue Faberge jeans and long-sleeved purple silk shirts, who had just started working on their shoulders. A large bowl of colourful fruits sat in a frame by the wine rack.

Angela lightly brushed her masseurs' hands aside and shook her head.

Joanne smiled and encouraged both the men to concentrate on massaging her. One began to loosen Joanne's neck muscles but he had to pause as she leaned forward and picked up a large bunch of red grapes. When the other masseur appeared from behind the bench seat moments later to work on her feet, Joanne handed him the grapes. She then produced a large hand-rolled cigarette from her bag that she lit and drew heavily upon. Joanne held the smoke in her lungs for some time before slowly blowing a thick cloud of smoke in Angela's direction.

Joanne motioned for the masseur holding the fruit to move toward her as she slowly reclined, resting her head in Angela's lap. With prompting the boy held the grapes just above Joanne's mouth, while his colleague got to work on her long legs. In between tokes, she swallowed grapes and smiled decadently at the ceiling. After she had passed the joint to Angela, Joanne began playfully stroking the groins of both masseurs.

Early in her career, Joanne had done several modelling jobs in Bangkok and she thought Thai men were remarkably sexy. Not just good looking but eager to please and versatile.

"Hmmm, I could sure use a little Thai comfort right now," she thought to herself as she felt the sex objects becoming aroused. She grinned suggestively at the fruit holder and used her tongue to manoeuvre another juicy grape into her mouth.

Angela was not quite as interested in the toy boys. She had less pleasant things on her mind. With a flourish, she produced Brett's Canon EOS camera from her Hermes Birkin bag and extracted the memory card containing that film. Angela waved it back and forth in front of Joanne's face. She gasped and sat up.

Then without a word, Angela threw the incriminating evidence onto the floor of the limo and proceeded to smash the rectangular black plastic card into pieces with her left shoe.

Martin checked out the drama through the mirror. "Here we go again," he thought to himself and smiled with anticipation as he turned on the microphone.

Joanne, mouth still wide open, pushed the grapes aside and gestured for both Thai men to move to the back of the limo. She laid her best 'I'll make you happy' grin on her friend.

On top of the remnants of the memory card, Angela hurled Brett's camera down onto the deck and, this time, used both her feet to thoroughly pulverise the instrument of Joanne's enslavement.

Joanne put her arm on Angela's shoulder. "Was that what I think it was Ang?" she asked with an admiring smile on her face.

"Oui" Angela replied and handed her the joint.

"So how, exactly, did you get Brett's camera?" Joanne inquired wide-eyed.

"Yesterday I went to le football ground before training and I took it from 'eem," Angela recalled.

"He, like, gave you the camera?" Joanne asked disbelievingly.

"Non, Joey. I kicked the pig in the groin, yes, then while 'eee was lying on the ground I ran away with 'ees camera."

Joanne's jaw dropped open and she smiled joyfully at Angela. A magic wave of unconditional love pulsed through her body for the second time that day.

"I can't believe you took such a risk for me girl," she said, her voice laced with emotion and husky raw.

Joanne gently took both Angela's hands in hers and stared dreamily into her eyes. "I can't believe what you did for me on Hannah today either. What a sweet and special person you are. I have never ever known anyone like you, Ang."

"Without the other footballers help, I may not have got away," Angela replied matter-of-factly. Joanne passed her the joint

As Angela toked and explained what had happened in the LA Eagles parking lot, Joanne just sat there stunned, unusually stuck for words, smiling like the Cheshire cat. As Joanne spent a minute digesting this amazing news and feeling the weight of the world rising from her shoulders, Angela finished the joint.

"Oh Ang you're the best friend I've ever had. I've never ever met anyone like you before. You've changed my life. Honestly." She kissed her soul mate French style.

"Thank you, thank you, thank you," she gushed.

Joanne's aura glowed like a super nova as she kissed Angela tenderly, full on the lips. Angela responded by stroking her lover with both hands.

"How can I ever repay you girlfriend?" Joanne asked sincerely.

"By getting rid of 'eem," Angela replied without hesitation and took the Californian drama queen by the hand.

Like a crystal glass hitting a hard floor, the spell cast over Joanne was shattered. The idea of "happily ever after" exited her fickle mind just as quickly as the alien concept had arrived.

A wave of confusion and panic and denial swept instantly through Joanne's wobbly head. It had taken just five heartfelt words and the fabric of her soul was stretched and torn. Again.

"I don't know about that," she muttered defensively.

"I do not want 'eem inside our new house. I want you to promise me that," Angela demanded.

Joanne hesitated and Angela scowled, withdrew her hand and slid backward across the fine black leather seat away from her.

"OK, Ang, OK. I owe you girl. I love you, I really do. Things will be different from now on. I promise."

Joanne smiled professionally, moved purposefully towards Angela and held her tight and long.

"I promise girlfriend," she repeated, then closed her eyes.

A minute later, she opened her eyes to find Angela still staring unhappily at her.

"Me so horny, Ang. Do you think these boys are straight?" she asked pointing at the masseurs. "Why don't we get a suite and go play with them. What do you think? Ang? My mind, I'm so horny, I can't think of anything else right now."

Angela shook her head impatiently.

"Ang? Earth to Angela! Hello?" Joanne moaned while slipping back into valley girl mode.

Angela sulked; pushed Joanne's hands away and ignored her friend's predictable attempts to change the subject.

"Hello, Angela? Please, Ang, don't shut me out. Please don't. I need you tonight."

Angela grabbed Joanne's hand and spun around on the bench seat to face her.

"Don't you change the subject, yes? How could you be sleeping with 'eem again, Joey, even after 'eee blackmailed you? Even after 'eee hurt you."

"Because he is so sad and sorry and lonely and ..." Joanne started to reply but, for the very first time, Angela began to seriously lose her temper and pretended to slap Joanne's face.

"That's the same bullshit story he gave you last time and the time before that, yes. 'Eee has brainwashed you," Angela screamed at her friend.

Joanne, who had never really seen Angela angry before, was shocked. She released Angela's hand and straightened her spine. Her head tilted back.

"You do not understand the beautiful little boy inside, he is so-oh misunderstood."

Angela responded with a sarcastic laugh and a shake of her head. Joanne's face hardened. Her head wobbled.

"Brett is shy, he does not trust people ... and he's the best, sexually, believe me, no-one else comes close," she said in a cruel, taunting and entitled tone.

It was a self-serving lie Joanne maintained to all her friends.

But Angela felt revulsion and disbelief from head to toe. "So what are you saying about me? Does our relationship mean nothing to you?" she thought. She felt like she had just swallowed poison and was going to die.

Subconsciously, Angela had clenched her hands into fists. The colour started to drain from her cheeks as Joanne retreated further into her hard-shelled la la land.

"Spare me, Joey, please," Angela yelled indignantly. "So what was all that talk with 'Annah about? What goes on in your mind, I cannot understand, yes."

Martin glanced in the mirror.

"This scene is more *Melrose Place* than *The Young and the Restless*," he thought to himself as his eyes darted back and forth between the busy road and the mirror.

Joanne shrugged brattishly at Angela and pulled back some of the limo's thick black side curtains with her left hand.

The moment she looked out the tinted window she saw Jenna Cheney - pale faced, pin-eyed, red-lipped and dressed in a black Dolce & Gabbana miniskirt and baby doll top, black fishnet stockings and red Jimmy Choo pumps - loitering with intent with two fat and ugly men outside the offices of Stallion Adult Films.

"Oh my god Ang! Ang, quick, check out Jenna's new porn gig," Joanne bitched like the excitable valley girl she was. "That is going to be a big story, we had better warn Reggie."

Angela placed her index finger to Joanne's lip and took her hand away from the curtains.

"Stop 'eet. Please. Look at me Joey. Please. Joey you don't need 'eem anymore. You don't. You deserve someone with love in their heart ... and you could 'ave anyone."

Joanne fiddled with her phone. Angela paused and waited until her friend looked up at her.

"You told 'Annah that I am helping you get clear of 'eem and I wish you would let me do that."

Angela threw her arms protectively around Joanne. "'Eee is like some kind of sickness that has invaded your soul." She said and kissed Joanne tenderly on the forehead.

"Where is the love in 'eem?" she asked in a quavering voice.

"No. No. Don't go there. Please don't, Ang," Joanne cried out and suddenly she started to weep and shake.

Brett was driving his hulk of an SUV along a freeway, passing a beach of fine yellow sands lined with gently-swaying palm trees. A mirror with two lines of white powder, a rolled $50 bill and a razor blade sat beside him on the passenger's seat. His mobile rang out a Jay Z tone and he answered it hands-free.

"Hello there," he said cheerfully.

The sound of gunshots, plural, screamed realistically out of his 13 Bowers and Wilkins speakers. Brett instinctively recoiled and pulled the truck out of the fast lane. An abrasive, filtered, voice crackled discordantly through the cabin.

"You're a dead man walking, cuore piluso. No one fucks with us, dawg face, no one."

Brett gulped and glanced hurriedly at the vehicles to his right and left - half expecting to see a gun-totting assassin taking aim - as the voice on the line warmed to its murderous theme.

"You kiss your mama the next time you see her, you fucking ugly pig. You kiss her and tell her how much you love her cos I got this feeling that it's gonna be the last chance you get."

More high-calibre gunshots and a blood-curdling scream erupted from the speakers and then the phone went dead.

Without warning, without looking, Brett swung his red truck straight across two lanes of traffic. It was a suicidal manoeuvre. A black stretch limousine had to break hard and swerve to avoid colliding with the terrified footballer's SUV.

Many horns blared but Brett - white patches popping up on his already seriously bruised and swollen black and blue face - put his foot down and with the pedal to the metal sped up a nearby off ramp.

Directionless, he raced away, desperately trying to escape the consequences of his actions, making another pointless attempt to run away from the toxic spirit that occupied his fragile mind.

Angela had her arms wrapped tightly around Joanne and was whispering quietly into her ear.

"We've made it Joey. We're Super Models now. The days of struggle are over. You will get the Louis Vuitton contract that you and Reggie have always wanted. All you have to do is stop sabotaging yourself."

Angela turned her head to face Joanne and the pair nodded. "You will find someone with love in their heart. You will."

Their eyes met. Angela tenderly stroked her face.

"Do you really want this mafia man coming after you?" she asked. Joanne looked blankly at her friend, blinked and physically shook.

Joanne blew her nose on a purple lace handkerchief Angela had handed her. She then shook her head vigorously. "No, you've got it wrong. That mafia stuff is all just one big misunderstanding."

Angela sighed and slowly shook her head.

"No, listen to me Ang. You weren't there. Brett told me what really happened and ... a journalist who hates Brett broadcast the wrong story just to get him in trouble."

"It is always someone else's fault, have you noticed that?" Angela replied incredulously.

"'Eee is bad news. 'Eee is unwell. Seriously unwell. Reggie says 'eee is psycho, says 'eee should be locked up."

Joanne appeared shocked by Angela stating the bleeding obvious and her head wobbled about disconcertingly.

"And Joey, my love, I completely agree with Reggie," Angela added quietly, doing her best to maintain eye contact.

"'Eee is a sicko who has invaded your whole being."

She paused as Joanne's head sank forward.

"There is no love in 'ees heart," Angela reminded her troubled friend.

Joanne had her tear stained face buried in Angela's cleavage. Angela placed her right index finger under Joanne's chin and gently lifted her face up. She spoke tenderly yet ultra seriously, nose to nose, to the dazed and confused Model Citizen.

"I cannot bear watching what 'eee is doing to you Joey. It breaks my heart, mon amour. It is madness, yes. I want to know when you are going to get rid of 'eem?"

"I ... I don't know," Joanne stammered. Her eyes blinked repeatedly.

Angela sighed and decided it was time to draw a line in the ever-shifting sands.

"I do not want 'eem inside the new house. If you bring 'eem there, I will move out the same day. I will never speak to you again. I mean it, Joey," she said sternly.

Joanne looked away. She refused to answer. The rational part of her mind agreed with Angela and Reggie. But Brett had a serious psychological hold on her. The curdled mixture of fear, charm, domination, sexual pleasure and humiliation he dished out had conquered her.

"It's the right time for a fresh start, Joey, it's time for you to purify your heart," Angela implored her.

Joanne's psychologist would later tell the FBI that she was the victim of a form of Stockholm syndrome. Brett had imprisoned her heart and she had become the drama queen who loved her jailer.

Deep down, Joanne loved the fact that Brett could literally do whatever he felt like and get away with it. She loved the way he forced society to bend to his outrageous behaviours, his wild desires and insatiable needs. The self-loathing part of Joanne's personality really liked the way he refused to accept her petulant behaviour or bow to her ridiculous demands.

Without ever really understanding why, Joanne profoundly enjoyed surrendering to her alpha bad boy. Ruthless and rat cunning, Mr Football had taken that submission to the bank.

But Angela was furious and, at that moment in time, no longer willing to meekly accept the status quo.

"'Eet is 'eem or me, Joey, you can't have both," Angela screamed at Joanne.

The limo braked suddenly as a large red SUV shot across in front of the vehicle, dangerously close to them. Martin's skill probably saved their lives. But during the reflexive brake and swerve response he had used to avoid a collision, a tall glass of champagne flipped over backwards and deposited its sweet bubbly contents all over Joanne's lap. Nearby car horns sounded in protest at the recklessly driven Ford SUV.

"Fuck it," Joanne yelled and half jumped out of her seat, frantically trying to brush the crotch-invading fluid off her Marchesa frock with her hands. One of the Thai men offered to help dry her with a towel but Joanne, who had other plans, crudely brushed him aside with her left hand.

The diva was determined to seize this messy opportunity to change the subject and amplified an uncomfortable distraction by turning on Martin.

Joanne sat up and thumped on the thick glass screen between their suite and the driver's cabin.

"Hey, coal face, you've just ruined a 10,000 dollar dress," she lied at the top of her voice.

Martin, full of adrenalin and surrounded by lanes of tightly packed and fast moving traffic, ignored Joanne's childish behaviour and stared alertly at the hazardous road ahead.

Despite the personal abuse, all Martin could think about was how wonderful the three of them had been together just a few nights ago. He could live to be 110 and he would never forget how perfectly the pair had pleasured him when they didn't even know his name.

Yet today when he collected the Super Models from the ABC's Hollywood Studios, he remembered, the blonde had just looked right through him like they had never met before. The French girl had been friendly and affectionate but the Californian? She had issues.

"What kind of racist nut job is she?" Martin wondered.

Joanne punched the intercom button and loudly tried to project her delusions of grandeur onto him.

"Hey do not ignore me driver, or you will never work in this town again," she screeched.

It had no effect. A glazed, stubborn mask settled upon Martin's face.

Yes he was feeling hurt and a little angry but immersed in the intoxicating sexual energy that seemed to follow this pair of Model Citizens everywhere they went, he was also feeling seriously horny again.

"I just saved your life, you dumb bitch, you owe me another blow-job," he thought but he needed to work. So he verbalised nothing and continued to safely pilot the limo down the freeway. Martin glanced down at the bulge in his trousers as Joanne continued shouting at him. By ignoring the specifics of her hysterical ranting, Joanne's voice did nothing but turn him on even more. He remembered her sexual talents and smiled on the inside.

Joanne thumped the security screen too hard with her left palm and immediately winced with pain.

Angela rolled her eyes, smiled reassuringly at the Thai men sitting on cushions behind the main seat and then tapped her friend on the shoulder. Joanne ignored her and looked at the bruised base of her left hand.

"Just stop it Joey," Angela shouted. "You are not changing the subject again! Listen to me. Please. No Brett, that's house rule number one."

"No Brett! That's the only important outcome from today, Joey!"

The tantrum was over. Joanne turned away from the screen and sat down but looked far from convinced. Angela turned up Aretha Franklin's *Chain Of Fools* on the limo's iPod system.

"For 5 long years I thought you were my man
But I found out love I'm just a link in your chain
You got me where you want me
I ain't nothing but your fool."

"You never did like him," Joanne said curtly to Angela while avoiding eye contact.

"The hold 'eee has over you, it is so unhealthy, yes. Why don't you care about this mafia bad man?" Angela replied firmly.

"Look I already told you and, anyway, Brett is so-oh important that his friends will fix everything, just like they did last time. The mafia dude is an Eagles life member, alright, so the club will talk him around."

"I saw this gangster man on the television. He was furious. He was full of rage. There will be trouble, yes? Big trouble," Angela countered loudly.

"I think you are exaggerating things a little girlfriend," Joanne said, trying to deflect reality with her best Hollywood princess drawl. Her emotional co-dependence on Brett was like a blanket that she just pulled down over her head when she needed to block out inconvenient truths.

Angela shook her head in disbelief, laughed cynically and turned into a French valley girl. "You are so, like, in denial Joey," she said grinning but still determined to make her friend see reason.

The limo screeched to an abrupt halt and Joanne found herself wearing a second drink. With her hair matted and the front of her clingy red dress covered in wet patches, Joanne started to scream at her friend.

"Just shut up will you? I've fucking had enough ..."

"I wish you had had enough of 'eem, yes. 'Eee will be the death of you, why won't you see it?" Angela yelled back at her evasive, crotchety friend.

"How can anyone care for you when you don't even love yourself? Maybe you have some sort of death wish?" she asked Joanne. It was Angela's most cutting remark that day.

Joanne groaned on the inside.

This heartfelt observation struck her like an arrow through the heart and Joanne would never forget Angela's words of wisdom.

While the Model Citizens argued about him, Brett sat frightened and sweating at a bare white plastic table outside a rundown, roadside, Mexican trailer diner.

Gram Parson's *In My Hour Of Darkness* crackled loudly from over-worked old Panasonic speakers:

"In my hour of darkness
In my time of need
Oh Lord grant me vision
Oh Lord grant me speed."

Brett gulped down a shot of Tequila, looked nervously over his shoulder, glanced at his phone and checked his watch. Impatiently, he called out his order for another drink to the Sombrero-wearing owner who was busy serving tacos to a middle-aged couple.

"Hey buddy! Hey, given the speed of service round here, you better make that two shots, OK?" Brett demanded loudly and started to repeatedly click the fingers of his left hand.

In the limo, Angela felt an explosive rage rising again as Kate Bush's *Red Shoes* played.

> "She said put them on and your dream will come true
> But the minute I put them on
> I knew I had done something wrong
> All our guests at the dance had gone."

Angela slapped her hand against the padded leather seat in frustration. Outside, car horns were sounding all around. A muffled male-voice threatened to do something murderous in agitated Spanish.

"This pig, 'eee will be the death of you," Angela screamed into her friend's face. "You have such poor taste in men."

Joanne pushed herself away from Angela and rapidly slid down toward the other end of the seat. Her inner street fighter roared. She turned to face Angela.

"Hey, that's enough! Leave me the fuck alone. How dare you talk to me about my taste in men? You, of all people, Angela Durand. How many relationship fuck-ups have you been with involved in over the past two years? Hundreds? Thousands?"

Angela's digestive system was still struggling from the night before and, as the adrenaline generated by the Hannah show had subsided, Angela suddenly felt overwhelmed and defeated and tired.

"I can't believe how you change your tune, Joey," she muttered. And, with that, Angela farted. Loudly.

Joanne opened the window and fanned the air with a copy of *Vogue* and they laughed. Both friends were glad to seize upon this vulgar circuit breaker.

After a reflective pause, Joanne closed the window and Angela, with a heavy heart, stared pleadingly into her eyes.

"I could really use some toot Joey," she said affectionately.

"Me too Ang, I surrender." Joanne said softly and sincerely.

"No more shouting, girlfriend. Please. I hear you. I do, I do, I do."

Angela slid across the bench and touched Joanne affectionately on the thigh. She caressed the silky skin on her face with her right hand. "I care so much for you, Joey, je t'adore," she whispered.

Joanne turned to face her with a sad smile as Angela produced a small powder-filled plastic bag and held it in front of her lilac-covered stomach.

"Yes please, Angela Durand," Joanne said and kissed her tenderly on the lips. "Could you be anymore perfect, my saviour?"

While her friend poured a pile of white powder onto the limo mirror and chopped four large lines, Joanne briefly rubbed her damp dress with a white D.Porthault cotton towel. She held the absorbent fabric against her gown for a minute, then produced a Cuban cigar-sized hand-rolled cigarette from her bag.

Joanne and Angela puffed on the joint and hoovered up powder through Joanne's "lucky" $1000 note.

Angela removed some residue from around her friend's nose and the pair lay back on the chair and quietly cuddled as they finished the smoke.

Mission accomplished, Angela picked up a stylish curved bottle of vodka and poured two glasses.

"It's time to celebrate our success, just you and me French girl," Joanne whispered affectionately.

"Oui," Angela replied instantly, slid her head in close and hungrily kissed her friend like there would be no tomorrow.

When Martin next peeked in the mirror, the Model Citizens were passionately locking mouths and bodies.

Minutes later, Angela handed Joanne a drink. "Try this, mon amour, it's Uluvka, the Polish vodka that Francis had for our office soirée," she said.

Joanne swallowed her drink in a gulp. "Not bad. Hey, that bottle is, like, way cool," she purred. Angela took the opportunity to refill her glass.

Angela's stomach rumbled rebelliously as she emptied her first shot. She poured herself another glass of the powerful vodka and then passed the elegant bottle for Joanne to inspect. She half turned, smiled politely and motioned for the masseurs to step forward and join them.

Angela grinned reassuringly as she took one of the men by the hand and guided him onto her lap. Joanne placed the vodka bottle on the table and dabbed at the smeared mascara lines on her face with the towel.

"Joey, you asked if we can sleep with these boys?" Angela continued, sensitively touching the faces of both masseurs. "If you promise me there will be no more Brett, the answer is yes."

"OK, Ang," Joanne sighed and held up both her hands in mock-surrender, "you win."

Angela tenderly stroked Joanne's face as Joanne pulled the second Thai man to her side. Flashing a cheeky grin at Angela, she nodded. Angela patted Joanne's sex object appreciatively on the bottom.

"Ooh la la, you are both so very cute," Angela told the two passive Thais.

"Hey, I want this to be memorable girlfriend," Joanne said with a conspiratorial giggle and grin. And with that, she pulled a Sony A700 camera out of her bag, set up a tripod, turned on the camera and started to fiddle with the controls.

"Oh beautiful billion dollar camera, baby, I love you," Joanne sang as she worked. She playfully kissed the camera that had ensnared Adam Verucce, leaving her red lip print on top.

While the director hammed it up as she set up the shot, Angela's well-practiced hands poured and quickly chopped two more lines of coke. With the enthusiastic photographer still focused on getting the light and aperture settings right, she declined another snort so Angela consumed both lines.

She looked up blinking and took a few deep breaths as the drug jumped into her blood and buried the last traces of her monster hangover.

"Ooooooohh, that's better," Angela said to the passive masseur with a friendly smile and kissed him on both cheeks and then slowly, seductively, on the lips.

"Hmmmmm, you are cute, yes," she said breathily to the luckiest Thai in the whole wide world. He finally relaxed and smiled shyly at his new friend. Angela took his right hand and respectfully kissed it.

Euphoria washed over Angela. Her eyes glazed and her jaw slackened. She took the masseurs left hand and placed it high on her stockinged thigh. She started to gently stroke the front of his jeans.

"Let's get a suite Joey. Shall we go that 'otel in Beverly Hills?"

Joanne finished programming the camera before she replied. "The Peninsula? Sounds like an awesome plan, Ang."

Angela pushed the intercom button beside the seat. "'Ello driver, can you please take us to the Peninsula 'otel in Beverly Hills."

"Yes ma'am," Martin replied as professionally as he could manage in the circumstances. "The traffic is real heavy, so the estimated journey time will be, um, around 20 minutes with one right turn," he added.

"That's fine, thank you, we are in no rush, yes," Angela said and clicked off the intercom. Martin nodded his hat obligingly and smiled on the inside.

Joanne smoothed shut the curtains on the screen and side windows, as the limousine made a gentle turn to the right.

Angela selected a Beach Boys compilation on the iPod and cranked up the volume as *California Girls* filled the space.

"Wish they all could be California Girls
The west coast has the sunshine
And the girls all get so tanned
I dig a French bikini on the wild island girls
By a palm tree in the sand."

And the foursome, finally, got down to the serious business of fun.

The girls cheerily hammed it up for the camera. Joanne produced and ironically shook her Estee Lauder winner's sash like a college cheerleader.

Angela hitched up her dress and did an improvised can-can style dance to the classic Beach Boys soundtrack. She rhythmically threw her legs high up into the air while Joanne and the boys watched, entranced,

They consumed her stunning flash and tease show in silence but the toy boys greeted its completion with excited applause and ecstatic smiles.

Angela bowed slowly and she and Joanne exchanged knowing looks as she lowered her torso back onto the seat.

The next sound Martin heard was of a zipper being undone, followed by Joanne and Angela giggling. Angela turned a side light off and, in silhouette, dragged her Thai friend down to lie horizontal with her on one end of the bench.

The sound of another zipper being opened followed. "What did you say your name was again?" Joanne asked her masseur. Before he could answer, she kissed him and hurried to extract his cock from his underpants.

Angela's giggles filled the space. Martin still felt a connection, even though curtains now blocked the rear view mirror. He could hear girl on girl action. Girl on boy action. "Is there any room for me in the mix," he wondered hopefully.

Martin pushed a button that activated a wide-shot camera hidden in the rear cabin and suddenly he could easily watch the amorous group scene on a small screen low down under the dashboard by his cramped front seat.

He gazed, enthralled again, as Joanne and both Thai men playfully licked trails of white powder from Angela's bare breasts. "Ooooooohh, oui, oui," she moaned with pleasure.

The limousine moved slowly on toward the presidential suite in Beverly Hills but Martin had real trouble concentrating. His two blood-shot eyes constantly darted back and forth between the small screen and the traffic-laden road that stretched out ahead of him.

Joanne moaned with pleasure as Angela and the two masseurs took turns to slowly, sensually, lick trails of toot from her rippling upper thighs ...

It was at 4.45PM Wednesday, three days before Super Bowl, that Reggie made his strategically planned move to protect his girls, his investment and his agency.

Despite his lawyer's serious concerns and shrill warnings about the consequences of taking the law into his own hands, Reggie knew exactly what he was doing when he climbed into his blue hybrid Honda Civic CUT sedan and drove out to the LA Eagles football ground.

Truth be told, Reggie had been visualising this scenario over and over in his mind for months. He had known intuitively this day had to come. It was just a question of when.

For the past days he had spent at least four hours each day practicing his lethal high-kicks at the dojo and Reggie had thought of little else. He had stuck a picture of Brett's face on his home maxi kick bag and his hours of side-kick drill had been so powerful and relentless that his friendly neighbour had, for the first time, made a complaint about a "constant thumping noise."

Whatever the consequences might be, Reggie was planning on "fixing" Brett Farrell once and for all.

"I should have done this a year ago," he told the nervous lawyer. "If I wind up in jail, so be it. Jo-anne's life is in real danger and I'm just like her Uncle Reggie. I'm looking out for my girl. She's like a babe in the woods and he has cast some kind of dark spell over her."

The lawyer could understand Reggie's point of view, even if she could not professionally agree with his proposed solution.

"She is all alone in this predatory fucking town and I'm prepared to do whatever it takes to get my girl out of harm's way. It's my job. I know the risks involved but this has got to be done right and ... no one else can do it for me," Reggie told the Attorney purposefully. "It has to be me."

Dressed in loose fitting black Kung Fu trousers, a black Yoseikan dojo t-shirt, black Armani suit jacket and black Kung Fu shoes, Reggie bluffed his way past the security guards at the LA Eagles stadium gates by telling them he represented Brett Farrell.

He chuckled at the irony of his lie as he parked and then sat quietly stretching and meditating in the car for 15 minutes. In his mind's eye, Reggie was revisiting the Ken No Sen mantra that Master Mochizuki had taught him - advance strongly, with a reserved spirit - when he saw Brett, in uniform and carrying his helmet, jog slowly onto the field to join his stretching teammates neat the centre of the ground. That was when Reggie took off his jacket, stepped out of the car and strode purposefully onto California's most famous sporting arena.

The day Angela and Joanne had appeared on the Hannah show, Reggie had received a late night call from Angela. Very upset, she told him about a text message Joanne had received in which Brett threatened to smash up her face with a "brick" and make her "so ugly" she would never work as a model again.

While this was just the latest in a long line of threats Joanne had received, it was the final straw for Reggie.

So this sunny Wednesday was the day that Brett Farrell would be judged and the content of his character found guilty.

Reggie wanted to deal with the perpetrator of numerous crimes directly, man-to-man, in front of Brett's peers. Reggie wanted to profoundly damage his footballing reputation in the same way Brett had permanently stained Joanne's reputation in fashion and modelling circles.

After so many years of dirty deeds and lording it over LA with impunity - after so many years of wiping his feet on people - on this day of karmic vengeance there would be nowhere for Mr Football to run. Reggie knew that. In front of his teammates, there would be nowhere for Brett to hide.

Coach Hemline, a tall solidly built man, frowned when he noticed Reggie walking directly toward the group of players and jogged over to confront him.

"This is a restricted area, sir, I must ask you to leave," the LA Eagles coach said assertively and waved his arms at three security guards standing 200 metres away by the players entrance.

The player security detachment were so focused on seducing two cute young blonde marketing interns, they had their backs turned to the playing field and did not register their coaches' desperate need for assistance until it was too late.

At this fateful moment, the LA Eagles assistant coach blew his whistle and led the players on a fast run towards the far touchdown line. Brett, who was having a shoulder strap adjusted by the team physiotherapist, stayed in the centre of the ground with his helmet sitting on the turf beside him.

"You best stay out of this coach," Reggie replied softly. But Coach Hemline, 6 foot 6 inches tall, strong as an ox and fit as a sprinter, was not having any of that. He followed his instinct, ignored Reggie's advice, stepped in front of Mr Model Citizens and blocked his progress.

Coach Hemline stood there, hands on hips and looked down disapprovingly at the smaller intruder. "You must leave the ground. Now," the famous Coach said menacingly.

Seconds later, Reggie's right foot swept both of Hemline's feet out from underneath him while Reggie's left hand simultaneously pushed through his right shoulder and Coach Hemline fell backwards, surprisingly gently, onto the grass.

"I'm so sorry, sir, I have no desire to hurt you." Reggie said softly but firmly as he looked down at the head of the shocked big man now lying prone, flat on his back.

"But this is a personal and professional matter that won't wait. Farrell has threatened my girl, he has cost me $30 million," Reggie said and, with that, he flicked Coach Hemline his business card and turned and walked straight toward Brett Farrell.

"Oh for fuck's sake Farrell, not again," Coach Hemline muttered to himself as he glanced at Reggie's Model Citizens Inc card. He jumped up and again waved frantically at the unprofessional security posse, glanced over his shoulder and saw that Reggie had reached Brett and the physio was running from the ground.

The coach turned on his heels and ran as fast as he could towards the cavalry.

"Fuck off Reggie, you don't scare me buddy," Brett yelled and ran chin-first at him. He threw a combination high punch and low front kick at the smaller man. Reggie easily ducked under the punch, blocked the kick with a bone-bruising blow to Brett's right shin with his left arm and counterpunched. His right fist hit Brett in the stomach and knocked the wind right out of Mr Football's lungs.

"If you ever come anywhere near my girls again, you piece of fucking white trash, your footballing days are over, that's my promise to you," Reggie said slowly as he stood and eye-balled the gasping big man wearing the LA Eagles number 1 jumper.

"You come anywhere near Joanne again and I'll break both your knees so good you'll never play football again," Reggie added quietly before he snap kicked the football legend in the groin.

He made a point of not driving the kick all the way home because, like a cat playing with a mouse, he was not finished yet. Brett groaned and as his head and chest lurched forward, Reggie turned his hips and reverse punched him clinically in the stomach. Brett made a whining noise like a balloon deflating under pressure and vomited out a triangular stream of frothy grey liquid, some of which landed on the cuff of Reggie's trouser leg and left shoe.

Brett's teammates were now watching on, open-mouthed, from some distance away. It was obvious to Reggie that not one of the other LA Eagles players had any intention of coming to the aid of their big name teammate.

What happened that afternoon had been a long time coming. It was Brett's karmic chickens coming home to roost and it wasn't just Thommo, Buddy and GW who knew it.

The LA Eagles senior player group knew Brett Farrell's behaviour had become psychopathic after his 2007 head injury but because he won the team Super Bowls and attracted hundreds of millions of dollars of sponsorship money to the club, they had to tolerate him. The players clearly did not like him. They obviously did not respect him. But they put up with Mr Football's constant anti-social behaviour because it was a contractual obligation. It went with the territory.

Besides, the pragmatic football players knew better than most people what a powerhouse man hell-bent on revenge looked like. They knew the difference between a genuine hard man and a pretender. So faced with Reggie's cold and focused fury, they made the right collective decision and stood back and watched.

As Reggie glanced down at the foul-smelling liquid mess on his shoe and trouser leg, Brett wobbled around on frozen feet in front of him. His hands were up, his fists were clenched, but his narcissistic eyes were full of fear.

"You should not have messed up my best party shoes, you fucking animal," Reggie taunted the footballer and launched a round house kick. As he rocked back on his left foot and swung his right hip forward, the top half of Reggie's right foot crashed into the side of Brett's already badly bruised face, breaking his nose, fracturing his cheekbone and sending three of Mr Football's coke-stained front teeth flying out of his mouth and onto the turf.

Reggie's perfectly executed kick knocked Farrell out cold. His knees crumpled beneath him and he fell unconscious in a bloodied heap on the perfectly manicured green grass.

Coach Hemline sprinted back to the scene with three wheezing security guards wearing blue jeans, black LA Eagles polo shirts, matching baseball caps and black wraparound Ray Ban sunglasses not far behind. The goons immediately drew their pistols and pointed them at Reggie.

He spun around to face them. Undaunted. Perfectly balanced.

"That's enough," the coach instructed the man from Model Citizens but Hemline was at least 30 seconds too late.

"You keep your fucking animal on his chain or next time I will break both his knees so good he will never play football again," Reggie snapped in reply and moved to walk away from the guards and the coach as - mission accomplished - he now wanted to leave.

The security guards locked and loaded their shining silver weapons and all three of them jumped in front of Reggie. As Reggie confidently eyeballed the goons, the guns and the coach, only two of the players walked up to support Coach Hemline during the face-to-face confrontation.

While Reggie pointed the index finger of his right hand at the small group, he directed his message specifically to Coach Hemline.

"Here's the thing, coach. If I am not back at my office within an hour, my PR chief will automatically call a media conference to announce that my lawyer has applied for 27 State and Federal warrants for your psycho pig's arrest. The charge sheet includes three counts of uttering death threats, seven counts of kidnapping, three counts of blackmail, five counts of rape, three counts of sexual assault, four counts of assault and narcotics trafficking."

The security guards looked grimly at the coach who suddenly felt the 2009 Super Bowl trophy slipping from his grasp. His breathing became erratic and noisy. His usually jovial face contained one big frown.

"Make no mistake coach, this ain't no bluff. My Uncle is the LA County District Attorney and he already has the paper work," Reggie continued in his reasonable and considered negotiator's tone.

"I promise you Brett Farrell will be indicted and in jail for Super Bowl. I wonder how the Eagles are going to win without Mr Football? Do you think you can do that coach? Do you think the fans will understand? Do you think the sponsors will understand?" Reggie asked without a trace of anger or emotion in his voice.

Confused, doubtful and demoralised by the rapidly evolving drama, Coach Hemline wiped his dry pinched lips with the palm of his right hand.

"Please think carefully," Reggie continued in his best deal making tone. "Is that what you really want coach?" he asked as he assertively eyeballed the coach.

"No, no, that's not what I want sir." Coach Hemline replied and moved his right hand, palm down, through the air in the direction of his security people.

"You make sure he stays away from my girls," Reggie said as he pointed his left foot at the wreck of a man lying on the turf in the blood splattered number 1 jersey.

"You make sure he leaves Joanne alone or, I promise you, I will be back to fix both his knees. Permanently. You got that?"

"Yeah, yeah, I got it," the coach said, his cracking voice betraying his distressed state of mind as he replied to Reggie who was standing just two feet away, staring intently at him with searing tiger's eyes.

"Let him go, let him through," Coach Hemline said firmly to the security detachment and they lowered their pistols and stepped aside.

Light on his feet, Reggie turned and walked slowly and steadily back across the grass towards his car. As he rhythmically walked away from the lion's den, not once did Mr Model Citizens look back at the shell-shocked group of slack-jawed large men he had left gathered around the ailing king of football.

Brett Farrell had not moved and was still lying exactly where he fell. Having checked his pulse, the coach pulled out his cell phone and, in his haste to summon the club doctor, twice misdialled the number.

"Doc Johnson," the coach eventually said into his phone. "Coach Hemline here, we have had another Farrell situation go down. Yeah. At training. Please come out onto the ground right now. Yeah, I know, during training, yeah. Please hurry and bring your paramedics and oxygen, he's not in a good way."

The coach paused, glanced at Brett and listened. "No. No, it's not narcotics related. Yeah, I checked Doc, he's still breathing and his pulse is steady," he barked into the phone.

"What? No. No. He just had the shit kicked out of him by some martial arts tough guy. No, no, it's not mafia related."

The LA Eagles players listened to the conversation and looked uncomfortably at each other. "No. I know Doc. No, it was some-fucking-thing to do with one of his model girl friends," Coach Hemline grumbled.

Buddy and Thommo rolled their eyes at each other and shrugged their padded shoulders to the wider group of watchful yet silent players. Super Bowl 2009 was only three days away and the circus had to move on ...

Reggie waved at the guard and smiled as he drove calmly out through the LA Eagles stadium gate and, with his adrenaline levels surging, headed for the office.

The following afternoon, Reggie instructed Angela and Joanne to meet Francis at Villain's Tavern, their preferred hangout near the agencies' Arts District home.

Francis had been given the job of telling the pair what had happened when Reggie confronted Brett.

Reggie had organised 24/7 security guards for both Super Models and Francis would introduce Angela and Joanne to their new minders, outside the bar, right after the meeting. That was the plan.

But the two men, two women, VIP security detachment got gridlocked in traffic caused by a Presidential motorcade and arrived at the Model Citizens building 15 fateful minutes late.

Angela and Joanne sat on purple velvet chairs at a spacious table, behind a tinted glass window that offered them discreet views onto the cosmopolitan street scene and an organic fruit and art market. Two cups of Lao coffee and a decanter of Saint-Géron water were set on the table.

Angela was completely focused on a phone conversation with her mother: "Mille fois merci."

She was wearing frayed and torn blue boho market jeans, a camellia-printed orange cheesecloth button-up shirt accessorised by the silver peace sign necklace, Birkenstock walking sandals and no make up. Her hair was tied back with an orange Tasha ribbon.

"C'est vraiment gentil de ta part, mama," Angela thanked her mother.

Joanne looked relaxed - wearing a sky blue Givenchy pleated Midi dress, red Anne Taylor crewneck t shirt and black suede Jimmy Choo Amy Court heels - she lightly tapping her feet to the bar's house music. She felt good as she stared out the window at blue sky and enveloping warm sunshine over a bohemian street scene.

Angela was seriously concentrating on the update she was receiving about the search for a new family home.

"Très bon mama," she said, giggled, and sipped at her coffee. As she listened, a contented smile spread across her face.

Her parents had found the "perfect" Château near Nice but they were worried that the €4.7 million asking price was too expensive.

"Just buy it. I will transfer the money this afternoon," Angela told Angelina without hesitation.

Joanne's iPhone rang. She looked at the screen, became tense and immediately stood up. "Hey Ang, I gotta go to the bathroom," she said.

Angela put her left hand over her phone and replied without looking up: "Francis is running 15 minutes late."

Joanne strode away from the table and around the corner before she touched the screen of her phone.

"Hello," she answered the call nervously.

"Yo slut! It's your motherfucking boyfriend here," Brett screamed at her. "Remember me? Wassup ho? Why haven't you returned my calls?"

"Just hang on one second babe," she replied defensively. "I'm just moving to a place where I can talk."

Joanne looked left and right around the room and noticed a couple of Indian Hills girls she had met at a Hollywood club three weeks before. They were waving and looking expectantly at her. But Joanne felt totally overwhelmed, ignored them and headed for the bathroom.

"Didn't she like just totally diss us, Alexis?" a dark haired girl in white Prada pants, red Lacoste shirt, fawn Coach bag, Chanel wedges and black Von Zipper sunglasses asked her friend.

"Yeah she did, Rachel. So-oh, let's go visit her. Like, I know where she lives. Her apartment is listed on celebrityaddressaerial.com" her sneering blonde accomplice replied.

Alexis was wearing a silver and black Asos Oasis cocktail dress, red Von Zipper shades that set off her hair and a Chanel enamelled gold necklace she had stolen from Paris Hilton's Hollywood Hills mansion.

"Hart is so-oh dumb, Alexis. Imagine flashing your tit at the Kodak like that," Rachel sniggered and fired a judgemental glare in the direction of the ladies bathroom door.

Behind the door, Brett was more out of control than ever before. "Why'd ya set Reggie onto me?" he demanded to know.

"I didn't set anyone on to you Brett. I honestly don't know what you are talking about," Joanne said as she walked into a cubicle and locked the door.

"You just lie and fucking lie don't you? You do know your psycho manager kicked the fuck out of me, broke my nose, knocked out three front teeth. I hope you're happy now? I just spent six hours at the dental hospital because of you."

"I'm sorry baby," Joanne whimpered, "but I never asked Reggie to do anything. You gotta believe me," she said anxiously.

"Trouble is, I can't believe a word you say," Brett spat his interruption into the phone. "And you know what the fundamental problem is slut? You don't listen to a fucking word I say. You don't, do you?"

He paused. His deep erratic breathing punctuated the silence.

"I warned you plenty 'bout what would happen if you told Angelina and Reggie about the films but you just don't fucking listen."

"I do listen, of course I listen to you sir," Joanne protested. With her right hand, she began to slowly rub her stomach in a circular motion.

"Why would I listen to your fucking ho lies?" Brett replied angrily.

"You go on national TV and say I'm your ex boyfriend. You tell Hannah I'm a violent thug. Your manager comes to training last night. Breaks my nose. Knocks my teeth out. Makes my head hurt worse than any football injury I ever had and you say it's got nothing to do with you. Do you seriously want me to believe that you dumb ho?" Brett screamed incredulously.

"But I have not spoken to Reggie for two days," Joanne whispered. "That's the truth babe. He sent me a text this morning about a meeting but ..."

"Shut it," Brett yelled so loudly Joanne felt her right ear drum pop.

"Shut your mouth, stop your lying and listen to me. Just fucking listen, OK. Listen real carefully to Brett. If you don't want your slut ass plastered all over pornland, listen real carefully to me."

Joanne placed her bag on top of the toilet's cistern and shut her eyes.

"You and your fucking titless friend thought it was pretty goddam funny stealing Brett's camera didn't you. But do you really think Angelina got the master tape? DO YOU? Don't be so goddam stupid Joey. See, I got cameras hidden all over the roof at home. I got cameras in every room. So I got all your sex slave training sessions on film. I got everything."

Joanne groaned out loud. Brett laughed cruelly and continued his verbal assault.

"Oh yeah. You're not so fucking clever now are you? I got your pretty ass on tape. You better believe it! You in your best little girl begging voice. I got most everything, including you blowing that basketball team! You do remember that scene, don't you Joey?" he taunted her.

"I reckon there's at least 60 hours of footage and since you dumped on Brett on the Hannah show, I've been real busy with a film maker friend of mine editing together all the best bits," he said gleefully and chuckled.

Joanne's bladder suddenly spoke to her. She pulled down her knickers, sat down on the toilet seat, and began to pee. It was a welcome if brief distraction from the total nightmare her life had just become.

"And you wanna know the good news Joey? Some good old San Fernando Valley boys have already offered me $2.5 mill for the footage of you. Way things are between us, I figure I might as well take their money."

He paused to let the threat sink in. Joanne just sat there pale-faced and open mouthed.

"If you don't come meet with me this afternoon, I will be sending your slut films to my porn buddies. They tell me their marketing people are, like, totally drooling. They're gonna slap your ho face all over the DVD covers and make a series called The Super Model That Loves Pain."

"No, Brett, purlease, no," Joanne begged.

He just laughed bitterly. "I warned you Joey. I fucking told you what would happen if you crossed me. So this is all your fault, you dumb slut."

"I don't want to play no games with you babe, I just want you to be happy," Joanne said submissively.

"Remember I got absofuckinglutely nothing to lose now. I'm already the big bad evil monster you sent your fucking thug of a manager to beat up, so don't play no more of your manipulative games with me, Joey."

She sobbed.

"Do you want the tapes or do you want Brett to drive up to the San Fernando Valley this afternoon?"

"No, purlease, no sir. I want the tapes," Joanne whimpered.

"Do you wanna kiss your precious modelling career goodbye? Do you? You know when this stuff hits the Internet your career will be toast. Reggie will drop you. Your clients will drop you. Your friends will drop you. Even that ho Angelina will drop you," Brett yelled.

"The only person gonna take a call from your sad ass tomorrow is a porn publicist."

Joanne shook her head.

"Is that the kinda future you want Joey?"

"No, purlease, no Brett. What do you want me to do? You know I'll do anything for you babe."

"What do I like you to call me?"

"Sir."

"Say it again properly then slut," Brett demanded.

"You know I'll do anything to please you, sir," she responded immediately.

"Well, there's only one way you can please your master today OK. You meet me at our beach in two hours time. At three o'clock. You tell no one. NO ONE. And you come alone. Understand. Try anymore of your ho tricks and the tapes are going straight on the Internet. You got that?"

"Yes sir, I got that sir," she squeaked obligingly in her best little girl's voice.

"Three o'clock. Don't you be fucking late," Brett screamed at her and terminated the conversation.

Joanne was white as a sheet, short of breath and trembling from the shock of being blackmailed but she had no doubt about what she had to do. She stood up, tidied herself up, left the cubicle, touched up her face in the mirror and rushed out of the bathroom.

Rachel and Alexis laughed mockingly as Joanne's tense frame hurried past their coffee and cake laden table.

"The tit flasher just moved to Venice and she, like, uses Twitter," Rachel said and sniggered as she touched the screen of her smartphone.

"Imagine all the bling and celebrity clothes she's got. Let's go shopping at her house when the Super Bowl is on," Alexis said and the pair high-fived gleefully.

When Joanne arrived back at the table, Angela was still talking to her beloved mother about the wonderful prospect of a new life on the sunny French Riviera.

"Hey Ang, sorry to interrupt but I got to go back to the office. Reggie's got the draft Louis Vuitton contract for me to look at," Joanne mumbled.

"Congratulations Joey," Angela replied with a fraternal smile and pointed apologetically at the phone.

"I'll call you as soon as we're done. I promise," she lied, kissed Angela quickly on one cheek and with that - not wanting her perceptive friend to pick-up on her deep sense of dread - Joanne raced out the door.

Five minutes later, Francis finally arrived at the Villains table wearing dark NYDJ jeans, crème Pleione Peasant blouse, a long black Eileen Fisher cardigan and crème Naot sandals. She hid her surprise when she asked Angela where Joanne was.

"Reggie just rang and asked her to go back to the office. Something to do with the Louis Vuitton contract," Angela said, held up her left index finger and mouthed "give me one minute" to Francis.

"À tout à l'heure mama. Je t'aime de loin. Au revoir," she said with sunshine in her voice and ended the call.

"Bonjour, Ang. Great news about Joanne and Louis Vuitton," Francis said quietly. She smiled her best plastic PR smile and leant forward and kissed Angela lightly on both cheeks.

"Can I get you something stronger than coffee while I am up at the bar?"

"Why not? We will 'ave a new house on the Riviera by this time next week, yes. So a double vodka would be nice Francis," Angela replied dreamily.

Francis dialled a number on her Blackberry as she stood waiting for service at the bar.

"Reggie, hi, it's me. Just wondering why you didn't let me know you'd called Joanne in for the Louis Vuitton deal?"

She listened for a moment and a frown spread across her face.

"Oh. Oh. We've got us a situation here. Joanne left Villains 10 minutes ago, told Angela she was meeting with you to talk about the contract."

Uptown, Giselle Richter took a call on her private line and immediately afterwards told her secretary she has "urgent private business" to attend to.

Dressed in a black Ralph Lauren lace bib cotton dress, sapphire necklace, Jonathan Adler print jute bucket hat, sapphire Estee Lauder lip gloss, black Miu Miu pointy toe boots and carrying an emerald green Fendi bag, she abruptly cancelled all her appointments.

Giselle ran from the lift and jumped into her customised silver Mercedes Benz S63 AMG and raced out toward Malibu where, she believed, she would finally get conclusive evidence that Joanne had rigged the result of the 2009 Estee Lauder International Modelling Awards by blackmailing Adam Verucce.

The "programmatic specificity" of the revenge process had been thoroughly calculated in Giselle's flow chart of a mind. Once she had shown the Super Model the blackmail videos on her cell and recorded Joanne's confession with the cameras hidden in her hat, she would force an admission out of Adam, transfer the 2009 award to Hannako, protect the Estee Lauder brand by proactively informing a friendly journalist about the scandal, ask the FBI to investigate and make sure that Adam's wife Cindy got a copy of both films.

Giselle's Private Investigator, Tony, and two of his associates had followed Joanne to a Malibu park near the ocean where, fearful and alone, she sat in her silver Audi TT Roadster coupe waiting for her date with destiny. Tony had immediately rung Giselle and she was now racing to the scene.

The Gale had luck with the city traffic and pushed her high performance Mercedes to the limit along the Pacific Coast Highway. She rendezvoused with the white van carrying Tony and his team 25 minutes later.

It was 3PM and Tony and his associates had just climbed into Giselle's idling car when Brett's red Ford SUV rumbled past them and turned into the parking lot. Peering through compact black Swarovski binoculars, Tony told Giselle "that's Farrell" as the truck came to a stop right in front of Joanne's Audi. Brett walked to her car, yanked open the door and dragged her out of the driver's seat by her hair. One of Tony's associate's began filming the unfolding scene.

Giselle looked quizzically at Tony and he said "we should wait here."

"No way, Tony. This is one time she is not getting away with it," Giselle yelled. As her nose twitched angrily, she clicked the automatic transmission into drive and put her foot down. The Merc swung around the corner, into the car park, and accelerated towards Brett's SUV.

Mario knelt down hastily in the sand dunes and peered down the long green tube into the crossed sight half way down the fat barrel of the bazooka. As his colleague Gino used binoculars to peer down on the pair in the parking lot 100 metres away, Mario methodically checked the weapon-ready light and clicked off the safety catch. His left hand gripped the forward stock and his right index finger hovered over the trigger.

"The guy by the truck, it's him," Gino reported quietly. "Take the shot."

Mario stared intently at Brett through the crosshairs, softly exhaled and squeezed the trigger. At that very moment, Giselle's car screeched to a halt just a metre in front of Brett, Joanne and the SUV.

A millisecond later, a 1.6-kilogram bazooka rocket hit the Mercedes amidships. The force of the explosion tore apart the car's front and rear sections - it smashed the roof and passenger's side panel - and turned them into fragments of flying metal and reinforced glass. The petrol tank exploded, incinerating Giselle, Tony and his two unlucky associates.

But the driver's side of the customised Mercedes stood tall. The precision-engineered bomb-proof panels and blast-proof glass withstood the deadly impact and diverted the wave of shrapnel and tsunami of flames up and over Joanne and Brett.

Somewhere in Stuttgart, Germany, lived a gifted design engineer who had saved their lives just two days before Super Bowl.

Joanne fainted in front of the apocalyptic inferno and collapsed into Brett's arms. Without hesitation he lifted her up, threw her roughly into the cab of the truck, dived terrified behind the wheel, hurriedly reversed away from the combat zone and then raced up the parking lot and turned, blind, onto the Pacific Coast Highway. Brett pushed the accelerator flat to the floor and fled toward the City of Lost Angels.

"Fuck it," Gino cursed as he and his partner watched the hit go wrong. Mario shrugged and casually threw the bazooka onto the sand. "Will we still get paid?" he asked and removed his bespoke black gloves and placed one in each of his jacket pockets. "It was Vince who wanted the big spectacular. If he'd gone with the machine guns, like we recommended, we woulda got the pig."

"Cheer up, my friend. The Don will pay up and he'll give us another contract," Gino replied breezily and slapped Mario on the back. The pair of short solidly built men in black glanced fleetingly at the flaming wreckage below, then scrambled over the sand dunes, down onto the beach and made good their escape.

Four hours later, Joanne awoke, to find herself barefoot, gagged and chained to a queen-sized bed in a room in a seedy South Central motel. Her ears were still ringing from the explosion.

Brett had chosen a crack dive, the kind of place where, he knew from experience, a $100 tip at check-in guaranteed no one asked awkward questions or remembered anything.

Joanne's nose registered the horrid smell of singed hair and barbecued skin that filled the room. As he sat at the end of the bed, she could see that what little hair Brett had left on the back of his head had been burnt. "My eyebrows feel real strange," she thought.

Gram Parson's *Still Feeling Blue* played on Brett's iPhone.

"Time can pass
And time can heal
But it don't ever pass
The way I feel."

Joanne could see Brett was rapidly counting out bundles of $100 notes and methodically placing them into a large suitcase on the floor, to the left of his feet. Her heart sank low. Intuitively she knew right there and then that her rat was getting ready to abandon his sinking ship.

Joanne lay there quietly watching. After a minute or two she heard him mutter "$6 million" as, hunched forward, he dropped another brick of cash into the half full case. Right then, after he had cunningly spotted her open eyes, Brett strolled into the foul-smelling bathroom, rummaged around in a battered black vinyl bag and returned with a large syringe.

"Hey Joey," he said with a friendly smile and jabbed the needle into her left arm. She whimpered through the gag and wriggled all she could in chains that bound tight without cutting into her soft skin.

"Don't worry, girl, you and I are gonna be officially dead as of tonight," he said without malice. Joanne squealed, shook her head, and slapped her feet against the bed. "No, no Joey, we're not actually dying. No. We're starting a brand new life together in Mexico and I promise you I'm gonna take real good care of you," Brett said softly as his well practiced hand injected the contents of the syringe into her blood stream. When the job was done, Brett removed the needle from her arm and tossed the syringe over his right shoulder.

"I promise our life together is going to be good from now on," Brett said as he sat down beside her on the bed. He kissed her protectively on the forehead, like he meant it.

"I promise Joey," he said and tenderly stroked her face as Joanne drifted helplessly off into the deepest sleep of her life.

The day before Super Bowl 2009, Angela was rudely awoken in her bed at 6.30AM as Gita miaowed in her ear. Reggie and Danni, one of her new female bodyguards, banged insistently on her locked door. Angela awoke slowly.

"'Ello, yes, what is it?" she called out, groggily, as she got up and opened the door. Gita raced out into the living room. Paul Simon's *Graceland* played on her Bose iPod dock.

"She said, losing love is like a window in your heart
Everybody sees you are blown apart
Everybody sees the wind blow."

Dressed in a sheer purple La Senza silk negligee, Angela was surprised that Reggie was just stood there, head down, in tight black track suit pants, a long sleeved black t-shirt bearing an image of the rising sun and a smelly old pair of black Nike running shoes. He held a large bunch of yellow roses in his lowered left hand.

Reggie slowly lifted up his heavy head and looked her in the eye. "Sorry to intrude like this

Ang but I am here on an urgent matter that could not wait. Can I come in, please, we need to talk in private?" he said solemnly.

"Of course, entrez," Angela replied.

"No interruptions please Danni," he instructed the bodyguard.

Reggie entered the soft-scented room and Danni pulled the door closed behind them. Angela clicked on the door lock and then sat down on her pillow-laden king-sized bed.

Reggie just stood awkwardly by the yoga mats and big bay window looking out onto the Pacific Ocean. He was avoiding eye contact. His face was grim and tear-stained.

Reggie had never visited Angela like this before and she knew intuitively that something was very very wrong. After a minute of silence and growing tension, Angela finally summoned up the courage to ask him: "What is it Reggie? What has happened? Why are you here?"

He looked up, hesitated and drew a slow deep breath.

"Joanne is dead," he whispered and Angela immediately began to wail. For a moment, Reggie appeared frozen.

"Noooooooohh. No. No." Angela screamed in shock. "No, I can't believe this Reggie. No. No. Noooooooohh."

He dropped the flowers and threw himself onto the bed beside her.

"What has happened to 'er? Reggie, tell me, please, tell me," Angela implored him, face to face.

Through gritted teeth he struggled to reply.

"Farrell, fucking Farrell," was all he could manage to say at that moment.

"Ooooooohh, why wouldn't she listen? Why?" Angela yelled angrily and threw her distraught body against the pillows and thumped at the mattress with both her hands.

Reggie threw his arms around her from behind and stroked her hair as they both wept. Angela's body shook and convulsed, her limbs flopped about on her pima cotton sheets.

15 minutes later, Angela and Reggie lay still on the bed, thoroughly depressed, holding each other tight, as *The Today Show* news theme played on her TV.

Heroic football pictures of Brett filled the screen as the host's voice said "The LA Eagles preparations for tomorrow night's Super Bowl lay in ruins this morning. Their star quarterback, Brett Farrell, is missing, presumed dead, following a massive explosion and fire that destroyed his Mt Washington mansion late last night."

The two numb Model Citizens stared at the screen as NBC showed pictures of the smoking ruins of a once-palatial home.

The reporter's voice over continued: "LAPD officials, while as yet unable to confirm that Mr Football was inside the building at the time of the blast, told NBC this morning that a truck belonging to Mr Farrell and a car belonging to his girlfriend, Joanne Hart, were parked out front when a massive explosion destroyed the LA Eagles star's mansion around midnight Californian time."

Angela refused to accept what she was hearing.

"I can't believe that Joey is dead. I can still feel her Reggie. She is still alive, I know mon amour is still alive, I just know it" Angela gasped.

Tears streamed down Reggie's face too but he said nothing. He held her protectively in his strong arms and wished more than anything he could rewind the past 48 hours. "This is all my fault," he thought.

When the TV showed an old picture of Brett in his football uniform and Joanne in a Prada little black dress and red Jimmy Choo pumps holding hands - as they celebrated a victory on the field of some crowded football stadium - Angela and Reggie just stared bleakly at the screen in silence.

"Los Angeles Police Department inquiries are continuing but we have grave concerns for the wellbeing of both Mr Farrell and Ms Hart," a uniformed LAPD spokesperson, Lieutenant McPherson said.

"Despite very public threats he made against Mr Farrell just last week, the LAPD has refused to confirm their investigations are concentrated on mafia boss Vince Bellosace," the TV reporter continued as pictures from the Don's angry media conference filled the screen.

"Mr Farrell last week broke Mrs Bellosace's jaw during a wild brawl outside LA's Vertigo nightclub."

A close up of Vince's enraged face appeared: "After what's he's done to my Lola, he's gonna wish he'd never been born," the Don snarled.

"But," the male reporter said calmly into a branded microphone, "Mr Bellosace's Attorney says his client had nothing to do with the bomb blast at Mr Farrell's home. The Attorney provided NBC with a written statement this morning which states that Mr and Mrs Bellosace are currently on vacation in the south of Italy."

"The LAPD say they are not prepared to rule out a link between the bombing of Brett Farrell's Mt Washington mansion and the military-style assassination of Estee Lauder Chief Executive, Gabrielle Richter, near Malibu beach, yesterday afternoon," the reporter's voice continued, accompanied by pictures of the mangled and burnt-out wreckage of a Mercedes coupe.

"Oh my god," Angela cried out and pressed her shaking hands together in front of her face as the enormity of the events of the past 18 hours fully hit home. Her eyes widened, she tilted her head forward toward her hands and silently recited a little prayer for Joanne and Giselle.

"We're not ruling anything in or out at this early stage of our investigation," Lieutenant McPherson explained.

"Just one day before Super Bowl and football fans right across America have reacted with disbelief to the news," the NBC anchor said over pictures of Brett, head-bandaged, scoring the last-minute touchdown that won the 2007 Super Bowl for the Los Angeles team.

"Coach Hemline told NBC this morning that the thoughts of everyone at the LA Eagles were with Mr Farrell's family and friends."

"This is terrible news for the entire LA Eagles family. We will be dedicating Super Bowl 2009 to the memory of Mr Football, may god have mercy upon his soul," a grim looking Coach Hemline said.

As the coverage had clearly turned to football, Reggie reached for the remote control and turned off the TV. Angela rolled over to face him. Reggie took her in his arms and kissed her respectfully on the forehead.

"I'm so sorry Ang but I gotta tell you my top security guy checked with his LAPD contacts and both Joanne's and Farrell's phones were inside the house when the bomb went off."

"The cops told him they are 99% sure it was a ... mafia hit," Reggie stammered as he struggled to push the appalling words out of his mouth.

He held Angela tight as she cried her shattered heart out.

"I'm so very sorry Angela, I wish I could turn back time," Reggie added despondently.

The pair lay there silently in each other's arms - still, pale, tear-stained and united in grief - for what seemed like half of eternity until, eventually, his phone began to ring.

"Please don't leave me Reggie," Angela begged him as he sat up to take the call.

Reggie heard the words but it was the spiritual need and vulnerability he saw in Angela's eyes - and the mountain of guilt he felt for failing to effectively deal with the psychopath, the total responsibility he felt for Joanne's death - that finally ended two painful years of living in denial.

"I will look after you Angela. You are the most precious thing in the world to me. Nothing else matters anymore," he told her sincerely, maintaining full eye contact as he turned the intrusive Blackberry off and dropped it onto the floor.

Angela sat up, pulled him in close and kissed him. Her arms held him tight. Their bodies were pressed together as one when they fell back onto the silk-lined mountain of St Geneve Eiderdown pillows.

"I love you Angela, I always have, that's the truth," Reggie said softly as he lay upon his side and peered through his tears into her enchanting eyes.

Angela smiled shyly - loving and sad and profound - at her Model Citizen.

"I love you too, Reggie. I 'ave waited so long for this moment to arrive," she whispered. They kissed once more and Angela rolled effortlessly onto her back, spinning Reggie on top of her.

With both hands, she held his buttocks and slowly kissed up and down his neck. "I just wish Joey were 'ere to see us now," Angela told Reggie with a trembling voice. "You know, she always told me you were the man for me," she said, her tone overloaded with emotion, as she tenderly stroked his stubble lined facial features.

"So many times Reggie," Angela said as she stared nose-to-nose into his crystal blue eyes, "so many times Joey told me I should be with you ..."

The crushing sense of responsibility fell heavily upon Reggie again and he burst into fits of tears and anguished whimpering.

Angela comforted him. She cuddled him and carefully stroked his back until the pain had diminished a little.

Reggie leant gratefully in close and rhythmically kissed Angela on the lips, on the neck, on the forehead and, finally, full and lovingly on the lips.

They might have chased the nightmarish footballer blues away like two love-struck teenagers but at the end of eight tumultuous days, a stunningly beautiful girl with a heart of gold had blossomed into a wise and wealthy woman.

And Reggie? Reggie had grown up. In this time of senseless tragedy, he had finally become an emotionally intelligent human being.

"I know if Joey were here, she would want us to make the most of this moment," he whispered to his soul mate while ever so gently rubbing her nose with his.

"Yes Reggie," she replied quietly and, as her right hand caressed the side of his face, she stole his breath away with that dazzling billion dollar smile.

"Yes, Joey would want us to be happy together," Angela continued, her sad brown eyes ablaze, and then she kissed Reggie like she had never kissed anyone before ...

Enjoyed this book?

For more information:

www.asenseofplacepublishing.com

Printed in Australia
AUOC02n1051271113
258782AU00001B/1/P

9 781456 620141